The SCOT'S WARNING

Highland Hunters 6

KEIRA MONTCLAIR

Note to Readers

I THINK YOU'LL REMEMBER hearing about Ysenda and Lewis in The Scot's Vow, the story of Ceit MacAdam and Brin Cameron. Ysenda and Lewis were mentioned during the avalanche scene when things had started getting very interesting between Brin and Ceit. I couldn't very well stop and turn to Ysenda and Lewis at that moment, but I was certainly tempted! But then I wrote The Scot's Destiny, a Christmas novella, and Ysenda and Lewis still didn't have their moment to shine, and I knew I couldn't wait much longer. Now I'm finally able to get back to this couple who set my mind whirling way too early. But to do them justice, I've got to go back to where it all began: the avalanche in The Scot's Vow.

CHAPTER ONE

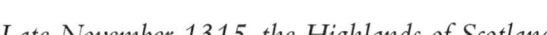

Late November 1315, the Highlands of Scotland

YSENDA RAMSAY HUDDLED deeper inside her mantle, with the odd thought that if she could, she would hide herself from everyone: the patrol, her parents, even her brother and sister. She'd been so excited for this patrol, the chance to prove her skills as all her cousins had done before her, but this sudden turn of events—a blinding blizzard—had changed everything.

Ysenda was one of those people who liked things to stay the same. She loved to fight as an archer but only from a tree. It was the safest place for her; at least, that's what her nightmare persisted in telling her. And the weather caught her completely off guard because she'd been expecting a skirmish. That was what she'd hoped to happen, another battle against the English, not the blasted weather. She didn't wish to be here in the middle of a wild snowstorm in an area she was unfamiliar with.

She was petrified—utterly and unequivocally

petrified. And the thought of crossing the ravine ahead made her wish to retch.

"Race ye across the ravine," Lewis Haggert called out from his horse behind her.

She rolled her eyes, glad he couldn't see them, but she was overtired with his constant attempts at banter. This whole situation gave her a bad feeling, the kind that conjured up the worst possible scenarios for a team of a half score people crossing a treacherous ravine in the middle of howling winds and blinding snow. She tucked her long plait inside the hood of her wool mantle, though strands of her light brown hair blew across her face.

She had visions of only half of them making it to the other side.

This was no time for jokes so she chose to ignore Lewis' foolish comment. She glanced over her shoulder at him, his hair shining dark red even in the snow, and beyond him, pleased to see they were not at the end. Ceit MacAdam was behind Lewis, with Brin Cameron behind her.

She narrowed her gaze, yanking the scarf tighter around her mouth to keep the ice crystals off her lips. She hadn't been thrilled about heading to Inverness in the beginning of winter, but she was here because her parents expected it of her, as did her grandparents, and her aunts and uncles, her chieftain. The list was nearly endless. She did it because she'd trained for this for many years. It was something she'd always wished to do. She did it because it was the right thing, to fight and protect your clan and all the lands of Scotland. She did it because the English were bastards.

She hadn't questioned this role of hers in protecting her country until the last moon. Fighting in warm weather was easy, but as the weather turned colder, she'd started to feel a bit dispirited. Never mind the battles, would they survive this storm?

The other problem she'd had of late was something she could do without. Her nightmares had returned recently and with them she'd started rethinking her life, her desires, her destinations. She had a recurrent dream of watching herself in an animal attack that would not leave her. How did one go about banishing persistent thoughts from one's head?

As unsettling as the dream was, she never was able to finish it, never able to find out if she survived the attack. It hadn't truly bothered her until now. This weather. This blizzard. This blinding, whirling, mesmerizing precipitation. Was her recurring dream some kind of premonition? Was she about to die soon?

Dyna was ahead of her and said, "Push ahead. We can make it. Stay directly behind me, Ysenda. We canno' delay any longer." With her platinum hair and the snow covering her shoulders and her mount, Dyna was becoming nearly invisible in the swirling flakes.

Ysenda nodded and pressed forward, wanting to keep Dyna in her sights. Dyna Grant Corbett and Maitland Menzie had led the band through multiple skirmishes and patrols already. They'd make it through this one.

Ignoring the spasms deep in her belly, she pushed forward, keeping her horse in line with Dyna's. As long as her cousin's steed was safe, then hers would surely be fine too. They moved through without any problem until they were about halfway across the ravine and an odd rumbling caught her attention, a sound that made her look skyward for snow thunder.

Unfortunately, it wasn't snow thunder. It was an avalanche.

She looked up just as Lewis leaped off his horse toward her, knocking her forward in an attempt to protect her from the landslide of snow and stone showering over them, bombarding them with a blast that she hadn't expected or experienced before.

They landed hard on the ground, the horses now rearing on their hind legs in fear. Looking back, she caught the sight of Brin grabbing the reins of Ceit's horse to control the beast while Dyna grabbed her horse's reins. Brin tossed Ceit away from trouble, the frantic lass landing on Brin's horse and out of harm's way.

Lewis landed off to the side of Ysenda, the two of them looking up in time to see an inundation of snow and debris coming for them, the momentum from the slide somehow sweeping underneath them and carrying them over the edge of the ravine. Ysenda flailed to hang onto anything she could but found nothing as she bounced several times off the edge of the ravine, each collision with the landscape forcing a grunt of pain from her lips. She managed to push herself onto her side so she could roll, protecting her head with her arms the way her father had taught her to do as she fell down the steep incline so quickly that it took her breath away.

A sharp pain in her leg made her scream, and she finally landed in a heap at the bottom of the gully as snow continued to fall, nearly burying her in its cold, wet tendrils.

When she was able to catch her breath and attempt to stand, she couldn't. Not only was she covered by the snow but her leg was unable to bear her weight. And right next to her, she could hear the rasping breath of an animal moving closer to her. The eerie sound sent chills down her spine and she strained to see where the sound was coming from, and to see what animal was stalking toward her through the packed snow and debris. It was moving closer. What the hell kind of animal was it?

This was it. She was going to die just as she'd been dreaming. Her nightmare was about to come true.

The animal's jaws were coming for her and all she could do was scream out in fear.

Lewis watched Ysenda go over the side. He had reached out to grab her as she was pushed past him but she'd disappeared into the ravine too quickly for him to so much as grasp at her cloak. He'd foolishly thought he could avoid the same fate but found himself catapulted over the edge of the ravine in a rush of dirt, stones, and heavy, wet snow. The only thing he hoped would save him would be the few inches of snow that might cushion his fall in some spots, but there was the risk of pain and injury from the stone and dirt where the soft snow hadn't collected yet.

Would he survive? Would Ysenda? Who else had pitched over the edge? What about their mounts?

He bounced several times, his arms protecting his head, before landing with a groan that ripped from his throat. Frozen from the shock for several seconds, he didn't move until he thought of Ysenda. Where was she, and how badly was she hurt?

Lewis tried to push himself to a standing position, but one arm gave out, that limb either broken or his wrist sprained, the pain too much to bear, so he released it and depended on his other arm to shove himself off the ground. The avalanche was slowing, only small pieces of stone and snow falling intermittently, which gave him the opportunity to look around for Ysenda and anyone else who'd fallen with them.

He didn't see her.

His heartbeat sped up the longer he searched, scanning the snow for a sign of her. Then he heard a muffled scream.

"Ysenda?"

He raced over to a spot where he thought the sound had originated from, kneeling down to peer into the uneven pile of snow and debris. "Ysenda? Are ye in there?"

He stilled, praying to hear her voice again.

When he did, he sighed with relief, yelling to her, "I'll get ye out. I'm here."

A glimpse of something darkened the snow, and he prayed it was her mantle. Digging with his hands, he shoveled and shoveled the heavy, wet precipitation over his shoulder until he hit something, and she yelped.

"I'm sorry!"

A voice from above bellowed, "Are ye both hale?"

"I am fine," he yelled back, digging in a different spot, a place he thought her face might be.

In another two moments, her face appeared, and she sputtered at him, "Lewis, I'm going to die. There's an animal in here waiting to attack me. What is it? Hurry. Get me out."

"I dinnae see any animal, lass. Could ye be imagining it? Mayhap it was the roar of the avalanche ye heard." While he wished to use his best sarcastic reply, their usual rhetoric, he forced it down, instead doing his best to comfort her. "Nay, ye'll no' die. I'll no' allow it."

He continued to scoop at the snow until he found an arm, freeing it up so she could help him by pushing at the snow that was covering her other side.

"My leg. I think 'tis broken."

"Broken? Are ye sure?"

"Nay, I'm no', but it hurts like hell."

"Give me a moment or two to set ye free, and

then we can check yer leg. My arm hurts like a bastard too, but I think 'tis only a sprain or a bruise. Might ye be exaggerating a wee bit?" He arched a brow and smirked, hoping to raise her ire. It was easy to do under the right circumstances.

"Shut the hell up and get me out of here."

He grinned, then leaned over and kissed her wet cheek. "Ye are back, lassie."

She gave a loud grumble but said nothing, trying her best to get out of the snow.

"Ysenda? Is she hale?" Maitland's voice carried down the ravine easily now that the constant noise of falling rocks had stopped.

"She's alive. I'm digging her out." Maitland looked more like a wee bairn, the distance between the two of them nearly ten horse lengths. How the hell would he get the two of them back up the sharp edge?

"I'm fine," she yelled. "But I think my leg is broken."

"Shite," Maitland said. He spoke to the others, but they couldn't make out his words. Then he shouted, "Can ye be sure about it?"

Finally clear of all the debris, Ysenda tried to push herself to a standing position, but the scream ripped out of her throat as soon as she lost her balance, grabbing onto Lewis to right herself.

"'Tis broken," Lewis yelled. "And my arm is worthless. I dinnae think I can get her up the side of the ravine with her broken leg by myself." A part of him wished to bellow, lift her into his arms, and carry her up the treacherous, slick ravine, but he was fully aware that if he tried such a foolish move, he'd find both of them flat on their backsides on his second step. The landscape was snow-covered with a slippery coat of ice.

Maitland yelled, "Dyna and I are going in search of a cart. Once we have one, I'll climb down and help ye out. Grif and Willum will stay here with the horses, and they'll help me when we return. Dinnae worry, we'll get ye both back up the side. I'm sending Tevis on to Matheson land with Isla, Wenna, and Thea. We may need their help."

Dyna called out to them, "Lewis, if ye can make yer way closer to the end, it may be easier to get ye out from there. 'Tis a smoother climb and not covered from the avalanche. Ye could sink into the snow too deep if ye try to climb here."

He peered up at the steep hill in front of them, pleased to see their horses were standing between Maitland and Dyna. Losing them would have been too much of a tragedy. All they had to do was get back to the top and they'd have a ride to Black Isle. His task was to get the two of them as close to the end of the ravine as possible. "I'll get her down there before ye come back."

The group disappeared, getting off the treacherous edge while the snow continued. He thought of Ceit and Brin, noticed they were not with the group. There was no way to pass the area they'd just fallen from, the avalanche covering the edge so thoroughly that it appeared as one. He couldn't see in the other direction because the snowfall was so heavy and there were too many trees, but he guessed the two were headed to the cave for the night.

Ysenda said, "Where is Ceit? Did she fall down the ravine too? I thought I saw Brin toss her on his horse. I hope they are safe."

Lewis helped Ysenda to stand and then stood on her one side to prop her up, so she didn't have to put any weight on her leg. He thought he detected an odd shape on the back of her leg below her knee. That seemed to be the part that was giving her the trouble.

"I saw Brin pull her from her horse and toss her over his own while he grabbed the reins of the animal. The horse skittered because of the noise of the avalanche is my guess, but I'm sure Brin saved it. I see no animals in the ravine, and no one else here either. Just the two of us, lass."

"They'll never get through."

"I heard Maitland yell to them to go to the cave, and he'd return for them after the storm ends. The spot where we fell is totally impassable. The cave is the safest place for them now."

Their movement was slow because the terrain was so uneven. Even without the snow, there would have been uneven land with rocks and brush. The snowfall was slowing, and he prayed it would stop, or their trip might only grow worse. But sometimes the snow felt more like rain, something he didn't like. Traveling on ice was a challenge for both horse and rider. "We can do this, lass. Take yer time and we'll get there slowly. 'Tis no' as far as ye think."

Together, they managed to get in about another six steps when Ysenda collapsed onto a boulder.

"I canno' go any farther, Lewis. What the hell are we going to do?"

He sat down next to her and took her hands, removing her hand coverings and blowing on them to warm them. One could lose body parts to cold temperatures; they all knew it. He had to keep her hands warm. Excessive movement stole the heat from your insides.

His gaze settled on something closer to the end of the ravine. "Stay here. I see something, and I have no idea what it is."

"An animal? Please, no boars. I swear there was one near me after I fell. Can ye see one?"

He glanced back at her, seeing the fear in her gaze. She wasn't just afraid. The poor girl was terrified of something. He had to calm her down somehow. Ysenda was granddaughter to the renowned Logan Ramsay. Lewis was nothing more than a Matheson guard, but he vowed to see her to safety. Not just because of her clan or because of his background, but because he truly had feelings for her.

Feelings he tried to deny because he knew they would never be able to be a couple, not with his background. Lewis had an unsavory past that he kept hidden from everyone.

He shoved that memory back, focusing on the present and their predicament.

He brushed a band of ice crystals from his short beard. "Nay, it's no' moving so it canno' be an animal, but I must see what it is. It could help us. I'll be right back." He let go of her hands and she covered them again.

He stepped forward carefully, looking for the best way to make a path in the snow. If he could find a line without rocks, flatten the snow into a path, then it would surely make their trek easier.

He reached the odd object and dusted off the snow before trying to pick it up. Saints above but someone was watching over them. His gaze drifted to the dark clouds over them at the moment. He had an overwhelming feeling like someone was indeed in the heavens, someone meant to see them to safety. Was it providence or a group of angels? This object couldn't have been more perfect. It was something he could definitely use to move Ysenda along with less trouble.

He whirled around and held the object up for her to see.

"What is it?"

"'Tis a long board, long enough for ye to sit on easily. I'll be right back." He dropped the board and headed down to where Grif would be near the end. Once there, he saw two men working with the horses. "Grif. Have ye a rope?"

Grif whirled around in the snow. "Aye. Do ye have Ysenda with ye?"

"Nay, but I can get her here quite easily if ye have a rope." He looked around, pleased to see lots of tree branches. They looked strong enough to tie to the wood. He could slide Ysenda across the icy surface if he had a rope to pull with. Seeing Willum return with something over his shoulder gave him hope. "Ye found it?'

Willum shouted, "I have one. Da always makes

me carry a length with me." He tossed it down to Lewis. "Yell when ye have her. 'Tis difficult to see ye through the snow and the sun is dropping. We'll help ye when ye are closer unless ye need us now."

"Nay, stay and keep the horses there. I'd hate to lose one. I'll get her here, I think, on my own." He wouldn't risk losing one of the beasts they needed to get them to Black Isle safely. Horses didn't like storms any more than he did. And chasing one who decided to run away would not be welcome. He hurried back to Ysenda, not surprised to see her shivering in the cold. "We are all set now."

"What is the rope for? And the tree branches?"

He'd found two branches he thought would work and brought them along. "Ye'll see. Have ye no' heard of a sled? I think the Norse created it. I'll build something like it."

"A sled? What is it?"

"Ye've heard of the kind they build to slide down hills?" He carried the board over to where she sat, still staring at him but shivering a wee bit, her lower lip trembling. Once he was close enough, he set it down to study it. "Look, if I tie the rope to the branches in a triangular shape with the piece of wood for ye to sit on, ye will move better in the snow. All ye have to do is sit."

"A sled. I've never seen one. Though Papa has created various pieces of metal to slide down the hills in winter, they never looked like that."

"The Norse use them all the time. They will move nearly anything in the snow. All we're missing is the runners, but with the icy layer on top of the snow, ye'll slide across easier than walking." He put himself to the task, doing his best to hurry without making any mistakes. All he needed to do was get her back to the top. Maitland would find a cart. She'd ride to Black Isle safely then.

"So I sit on it? And ye'll pull me all the way to the end? Are ye sure ye can pull it?"

"Aye. I can do it with this once I tie it together. I'm pulling ye out of here, Ysenda. Ye'll see. Then when Maitland returns with the cart, we'll be ready."

CHAPTER TWO

YSENDA HAD TO admit she was more frightened than she'd ever been. Here they were at the bottom of a ravine, no way out, and darkness was quickly descending. She could feel the temperature dropping as fast as her hope. Her premonition of impending doom had been correct this time.

She should have listened to her gut.

But as her father would have told her, "That was in the past. Ye must help yerself now." Staring up at Lewis, his dark red hair wisping around his face even under his hood, she decided to stop bantering with him and just chat instead. She had no one else to help her out of her present situation than Lewis, and without a doubt, he'd never leave her behind.

This much she knew with all her heart. Her eyes misted at the realization of how much she trusted him. "My thanks, Lewis, for no' deserting me."

"What? Ye think I would leave ye? I'd no' do that. We'll get out of here. Dinnae worry, lass."

He fussed over his creation, cleaning off the

wood the best he could, painstaking effort that went straight to her heart. "I'm sure 'tis fine, Lewis," she said as he fussed even more.

"I'll not have ye too cold. I wish the sun were out to warm it a wee bit, but 'tis no' likely to happen. Ye canno' sit on ice, so I'll scrape it off. I'm going to clean the poles the best I can so they'll slide well. We'll see how it goes."

"How far is it?" The sun was falling quickly, another fact she did not appreciate. "It's so dark. How long before Maitland and Dyna return with a cart, do ye think?"

Lewis stared up at the end of the ravine, the sun barely visible behind it. "They both know many clans, and there are several within an hour of here. They'll be back before ye would guess. 'Tis why I'd like to get us to the end, if we can. Mayhap we can get up the hill if I can find some sturdy boulders to help assist our climb."

"But I canno' climb," Ysenda said, nearly in tears.

She was doing her best to contain the sobs that threatened to wrench out of her soul because the pain was so bad. The colder it became, the more her leg hurt, but then she recalled her grandsire's words of wisdom.

"Better to be in pain than numb. Ask Brenna. When ye can no longer feel, trouble is coming next."

Pain was good, but it would not help get her up the small hill at the end, though it looked much easier to climb than the incline they just fell down.

"I will get ye up to the top of the incline, lass. Dinnae worry yer pretty head about it," he said with a grin. "And we have two helpers. I can see Grif and Willum have already made it to the edge. I'm sure they will help us if I need them. For now, they keep the horses settled as we'll need them to get us both home, but once I've managed to get us to the end, they'll assist for certes."

She narrowed her gaze at him and then let him know exactly how she felt. "Must ye always put an insult with yer words? Ye never call me pretty. 'Tis a tease, at best. Keep yer insults to yerself."

"Ye think 'tis an insult? 'Twas a compliment, but I'll call ye ugly if ye prefer," he announced for all the birds to hear.

"Go ahead if it pleases ye," she said with a twist of her lips. No one had ever called her pretty since she'd been five summers old. She'd grown up to be a plain lass, and probably appeared more like an old hag after the fall she'd taken.

But then she stopped, noticing how red his hands were while he worked on the contraption. One even looked more swollen than the other. Had he hurt it and was ignoring it? She had to be more observant. Lewis knew exactly how to rile her up, and sometimes, she hated him for it.

He chuckled. "I thought that might upset ye. Good, ye'll no' be falling asleep on my watch. I must get ye to the end, and I need yer help doing so."

She snorted, knowing all he said was the truth. He set the sled down and moved it back and forth, tugging on the rope to see if it would hold.

"I think 'tis the best I can do, Ysenda. Can we give it a try before it's too dark?"

"Aye, I wish to move on. I'd kill for a cup of broth by a warm hearth and a blanket on my lap." She blew on her fingers in a poor attempt to heat them. Hellfire, but it was freezing this eve.

"I'd ask for a meat pie, but the rest I agree with ye completely. I'll set the sled here and stand on the other side of it to see if I can keep it steady for ye. If I support yer arm, can ye slide onto it?"

"I'll try my best," she said, placing one hand down on the boulder to lift herself up, surprised to find it manageable until her leg moved. "Lewis, grab my foot, slide it with my leg. It pulls verra strangely."

He reached out and did as she asked, and she let out an audible sigh of relief. "Many thanks."

"I'll prop it, so it will no' move with ye."

Once she felt settled, he pulled on the rope, surprised to see the creation move so quickly that he had to run to stay ahead of it. She squealed because it reminded her of sliding down the hills on Ramsay land in the winter, even though the land was flat where they were, the sled moved easily across the landscape.

"There's enough ice on the top to make it a smooth go, but only if I can keep from falling myself." He raced ahead of her, tugging on the rope and she jerked, but then they moved much better than she would have guessed. His boots crunched with each step, breaking the crystal surface of the snow. She hoped that wee bit would keep him from losing his footing.

In a moment, they were flying down the gulley of the ravine, nearing the end when they heard a yell from the top.

"I found a cart and 'tis ready for ye," Maitland yelled. "Can ye get up the incline?"

Willum and Grif came out from behind Maitland and flew down the incline toward them. "We'll help ye pull her. If 'tis comfortable for her, then probably safer than picking her up to climb. 'Tis treacherous in some parts."

The three managed to get her up the incline without much difficulty. She let out two echoing screams of pain as they made their way to the edge, but they were finally on top of the ravine again. That alone picked up Ysenda's spirits.

Dyna fussed over her, resituating her mantle and hood. "Ye have to stay warm."

"How long until we reach Matheson land?" Ysenda just wished for a hearth and a soft bed.

Grif and Lewis both spoke at the same time. "Two hours in good light." The two stared at each other grinning, but Lewis continued, "The moon is bright, the clouds minimal now that the snow has ended. We move on. Ye agree, Maitland?"

"Aye, we canno' risk leaving her here in the snow. No cave for us. The horses will pull the cart, we just need to settle her and prop her leg so it does no' move much. Otherwise, 'twill be a most painful trip for her. Sorry, Ysenda, but this is the best we can do."

"If ye can get me near Isla, Tara, or Brigid and near a toasty hearth, I'll not scream unless I fall out." The three women were all gifted healers, so she knew she'd be taken care of as soon as she arrived.

"Fair enough," Maitland said with a smile, lifting her out of the sled while Lewis guarded her leg.

Maitland gave instructions while Dyna and Lewis arranged her in the cart. As darkness settled in, so did the cold, seeping into her bones. But at least she was finally out of the ravine and wrapped in a blanket.

He nodded to Dyna, who mounted her horse and said, "Time to move quickly. We canno' make any stops. We just have to get ye to Matheson land, and ye'll feel much better. The others went on ahead, so they'll be awaiting our arrival."

Two hours. That was all she needed.

CHAPTER THREE

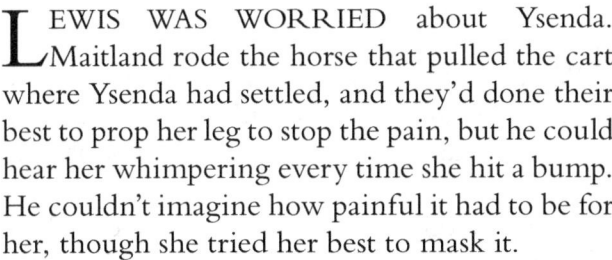

LEWIS WAS WORRIED about Ysenda. Maitland rode the horse that pulled the cart where Ysenda had settled, and they'd done their best to prop her leg to stop the pain, but he could hear her whimpering every time she hit a bump. He couldn't imagine how painful it had to be for her, though she tried her best to mask it.

"I wish there was more we could do," he said, leading his horse abreast of Maitland's mount.

Grif rode on the other side while Willum and Dyna took up the rear. They'd made it to the main path, and the amount of snow on the road diminished as they traveled. That could be both good and bad. The snowstorm hadn't continued across Black Isle, but there was also the possibility that it could start up at any time. It would be wonderful if they did not have to battle the snow, and the temperature would warm near the bay, but that meant the ride would prove rougher for poor Ysenda.

He was beginning to hear it in her voice.

"Maitland, there must be more we can do. She's in agony. If there's anything we can do to help her, please do it now." He couldn't stand listening to the poor lass. It was sheer torture for him, something that he didn't comprehend, but it was akin to raking your nails across a rough boulder. He could see it in her face and hear it in her voice.

Grif said, "Give it to her."

Maitland glanced at Grif and then back to Lewis.

"Give her what, Menzie? Ye must help her if ye can." Lewis was nearly at his wit's end worrying about the poor lass.

"We stopped at a friend's land who gave us the cart. I told him of the situation, so I also have a small container of the *breath of life*, should she need it."

Lewis couldn't have been more stunned. "Why have ye no' given it to her? Do ye have ice coursing through yer veins? Stop now." He had the vague urge to knock the patrol leader off his horse so he could find the amber liquid.

Maitland raised his hand, indicating he was not willing to stop yet. "Listen to me, and I speak from much experience, having known many healers. The *breath of life* will take most of her pain away, but it could also put her to sleep. In fact, it has the power to put some into a sleep they'll never awaken from."

"How could that happen? Most men drink it." He had to convince Maitland to give it to Ysenda to ease her pain. He couldn't bear to hear her in so much agony.

Dyna overheard and shouted, "Aye, most men

do. Most women do no'. Another one of those situations in life that favor men so women are at a disadvantage. Know that the amber devil has an unusual level of tolerance for some people, especially those who've never had it before. It also could make her colder. No one understands that principle, but it holds. Aunt Brenna told me that strange truth."

"I'll ask her if she's had it before," Lewis declared.

"Nay, I dinnae want her to know we have it until I'm ready to give it to her," Maitland said.

Dyna glanced over at her and said, "'Tis time, Menzie. She'll no' fall over. I care no' what Aunt Brenna says, 'tis no reason to subject her to such pain if ye have the power to ease it."

Maitland added, "Aunt Jennie says the same. She's probably never had it before. I was hoping to get halfway on the trail before I give her some just to get her home, in case she has any untoward reactions to it. She could fall sideways, roll out, and we'd never know it. Have ye thought of that possibility?" Maitland asked.

"Then I'll ride behind her. Or I'll even ride with her," Lewis offered. "I canno' bear knowing how much pain she is in. We must be able to do something. I'll do whatever it takes to help the lass. She's being tortured."

"Have ye ever ridden in a cart before?" Maitland arched a brow at him, though he continued to look ahead of them. "'Tis no' kind to yer arse, especially a man's arse. Women usually have more padding there. They tolerate it better than men."

This comment confused him. What difference would that make? "Nay, no' since I was a laddie." That didn't matter. It had to be easier for him than for Ysenda.

"'Tis most uncomfortable. But we are a wee bit more than halfway, so if ye wish to ride with her, I'll give her some. Just a bit to start, then we can gauge if she can handle it."

They both turned around to look back at the poor lass, and she squealed as soon as the cart hit a bump, her hands holding a tight grip on both sides of the vehicle.

"'Tis all I can stand. I'm stopping." Lewis stopped his horse and moved back to Ysenda, not surprised to see tears rolling down her face. "Lass, dinnae cry. Yer tears will freeze on yer cheeks."

"But it hurts." She gazed up at him and he felt an odd sensation in his chest.

What the hell was this lass doing to him?

"The landscape is getting rougher now that the snow has disappeared." Maitland dropped down and said, "Grif, ye and Willum keep watch for any animals. Dinnae let my horse move."

The two knelt down in front of Ysenda, and Maitland removed his gloves to swipe at her tears. He reached into a fold in his mantle and said, "Lass, Lewis is going to ride with ye. We are more than halfway there. Less than an hour should bring us to Matheson land."

"Nay, please dinnae move me. I couldnae stand the pain. Please, Maitland. I'll make it, but the pain is so bad. I'm such a wee bairn." She sniffled in the cold air.

Lewis was glad for one small blessing, the wind had stopped. "Ysenda, Maitland has a brew for ye to drink. 'Twill taste terrible because 'tis so strong, but it will also take some, mayhap most, of yer pain away."

"Give it to me. I care no' how it tastes. What is it?"

Her hands were both still in tight fists, and he swore there were ice crystals forming on her long lashes.

Maitland explained, "The *breath of life* from a fine friend. 'Tis mighty valuable as ye know. Have ye tried it before?"

"Nay, Da said he'd make us climb the mountain with no boots if we ever did."

Maitland contained his grin pretty well, but Lewis didn't even try. "Creative. I like it. So Maitland will give ye a wee taste, then I'll settle ye on my lap, and I'll keep ye from falling out. Mayhap we can prevent some of the ruts from bouncing yer leg. Will ye agree?"

She looked up at him, her mouth forming a perfect half circle of sadness. "Aye, if ye please. I'll be quiet. I promise. 'Tis nearly too much to bear."

Maitland pulled the flask out of his fold and removed the top and then held the tip to her mouth. "Just a wee sip to start. And if 'tis truly good, 'twill burn yer throat a bit going down, but dinnae worry."

Ysenda took a sip and nearly gagged but managed to swallow it. "I dinnae like it. Nae more." She swiped at her mouth but then waited.

"Come, we'll uncover ye, get ye on my lap, and prop yer leg again."

Dyna joined them and fussed with her, while Maitland lifted her so Lewis could climb underneath her, rearranging the extra plaids they had in the cart. Once he was settled, he motioned for Maitland to set her down, and then they went about propping her leg, something that took them a bit of time. Lewis caught Maitland's gaze traveling to Ysenda, probably looking for any changes, but if she noticed his scrutiny, she didn't say anything.

Dyna said, "Menzie, she can handle it, and she deserves it."

But Lewis noticed something had changed. When Ysenda leaned back against him, she had totally relaxed. Perhaps she truly trusted him more than he had thought.

"I like it. More, please." She grinned and reached for Maitland's mantle.

He stayed her hand and said, "A few more moments. Allow us to finish the task at hand, and if ye still wish it, I'll give ye a wee bit more."

She gave Maitland a lopsided grin and sighed. "Agreed. My leg feels much better."

"I'm glad, lass," Lewis said, patting her arm.

"I think Lewis likes me, Maitland. What say ye?" She let out a giggle and then stopped.

"I think we all like ye, Ysenda." He turned away from her, and if Lewis were to guess, it was to hide his smile from her. Ysenda was indeed feeling better, and Lewis was glad of it. "I think we can move ahead."

Maitland stood and covered her arms with the plaid to keep her warm.

"More please?" she whispered. "Just a wee bit."

Maitland pulled out his flask and handed it to her. She set it at her lips and tipped it back, taking a much larger sip than her first.

"Whoa. 'Tis more than enough for ye, lass." Maitland took it back quickly and then offered it to Lewis. "A wee bit to keep ye warm, Lewis?"

Lewis took a quick swig from the flask after Maitland turned back to his horse.

"Return it when ye've finished, Haggert, but be quick about it." He gave Lewis a look and then pointed to the bushes he was about to head into.

Ysenda tried to grab it from Lewis, but he held it far enough away from her. Lewis thought it would be better if he stayed away from too much of the proffered treat, so he capped it and tucked it away. "Nae more for ye. Ye've had enough for now, lassie."

Ysenda grinned and turned toward him, whispering in his ear, her warm breath sending a shiver through him. "But I wish for more. I always wish for more from ye, Lewis. Please?"

He chuckled, pleased to see the brew had definitely affected her. He'd never seen her openly flirt the way she was doing now, but he had to admit, he liked her this way. "Nay. I'll no' be fishing ye out of a snow drift. Ye'll roll right out of my arms."

"But I like it in yer arms. I promise not to tip over." Then her voice fell to a small whisper. "Do ye like me that much, Lewis? Enough to want more?"

His gaze narrowed, taking in her sweet scent, her long lashes, and the creamy skin that had turned a rosy pink, just like her lips. He glanced over his shoulder, making certain that the others were busy with their horses or off into the bushes so they'd not be able to hear his words. "That I do, Ysenda."

She wrinkled her nose up and said, "Then please give me more."

"Nay." He laughed just as Maitland returned, mounting his horse after taking the flask back from Lewis.

Their intimacy ended, he had to admit that he'd probably have visions of her sweet lips in his sleep. If only he could do as he wished, court her as if he were a nobleman deserving to take her as his bride.

The cold weather didn't allow him to think on that foolishness for long. "Cover up. We're about to start moving again."

She let out a deep sigh and leaned back against him. "Ye are much better than the cart." Then her eyes closed.

They moved on, the cold beginning to seep into his bones. Lewis couldn't understand how he could feel warmer on a horse than here in the cart. The going wasn't too bad, but every once in a while, they hit a big rut in the path. He did his best to absorb the jarring movement and not pass it on to Ysenda, but she was no longer reacting to the pain as she had before.

Thank the Lord above.

Her eyes fluttered open a while later. "I do like ye, Lewis. Do ye like me? I mean, no' like Maitland said, but really like ye. Have ye a girl who stole yer heart anywhere?" She spoke without moving, so he couldn't see her face to judge her mood, but he had to admit he was pleased with her words.

"I have no girls anywhere. No wife, no betrothed."

He didn't wish to say any more. He'd come to Matheson land only a few years earlier and he kept private certain elements of his past. He had never done anything of which he was ashamed but there were things about his life before he joined the Matheson guard that he did not wish to make known. Only Grif knew some of the truth because they'd come together to that homestead around the same time, and he trusted Grif completely.

"I am happy about that because I like ye. Will ye court anyone when the patrol is done? Wish ye to get married someday?"

He frowned, glad she couldn't see his face. She sounded as though she was deep in her cups. Did that mean he could trust her words, or was everything she said false?

He wasn't about to tell her the truth of the matter.

He was already in love with her, but he could never marry her.

CHAPTER FOUR

YSENDA HAD TO admit that riding on Lewis' lap was much more pleasant than riding on the cart alone. For one thing, he gave off more heat than the biggest hearth in the Ramsay kitchen.

She scowled, wondering what she had asked him. She'd forgotten already. Giggling, she had to admit that the *breath of life* was the best potion she'd ever had. Why, she could barely feel her pain any longer.

She wiggled her toes and lifted her leg, surprised at how easy it was. "Look, Lewis. My leg is all healed!" Lifting it up and down a few more times proved her point.

"Lass, 'tis yer other leg that is broken."

"Truly?" She stared at both legs, confused.

"Aye, try the other one, but just wiggle yer toes."

She could wiggle them, but even that small movement pained her. "Och, ye are correct. I canno' move that leg." She broke into a loud enough chuckle that Maitland and Grif both turned around to check on them.

Still giggling, she said, "I thought it was my other leg that was broken, but I was wrong. Lewis is so much wiser than I am." Her hand patted his leg to let him know how much she appreciated his help. Lewis was much more comfortable than the cold cart.

Maitland whirled his head back around to the front but called back over his shoulder, "Keep her awake."

She gave Maitland a sharp scowl, though he'd probably not see it in the dark, but why would he think she would be sleeping? "I'm awake." Why were the men sounding so daft?

"Good."

Grif chuckled and said, "Ye like Lewis, do ye, Ysenda? I think he likes ye too."

"I do," she whispered. Then a bit more loudly, she said, "I do, I do. Think ye he truly likes me enough to court me, Grif? Ye know him well." Then, she acted as though she were whispering to Grif. "He'll no' tell me aught about his feelings."

Lewis would have stood up and put a fist into Grif's mouth, but he was stuck where he was, and Grif knew it. He called a warning instead, "Never mind, Grif."

"But I wish to know," she explained. "Ye willnae tell me so I ask Grif. Unless ye are willing to tell me the truth of yer heart, Lewis. Are ye? Will ye tell me how ye truly feel? And please do so before we arrive on Matheson land. I dinnae wish for the others to know. But I promise, I'll keep yer secret. If ye tell me truly how ye feel, I'll never tell another soul. No one will be the wiser.

Except Maitland because he's right there, and he can hear us. And so can Grif and Willum and Dyna so that would be three more who know. Or would it be six? Should I count ye and me? So there are five who know the secret or two? But first ye must tell me. What is in yer heart? Who are ye most interested in? And please dinnae tell me Thea because that would break my heart. Because I wish to give my heart to ye. No one else is as handsome as ye. No' even Maitland on his horse is as handsome as ye." Then she giggled. "Sorry, Maitland. I dinnae intend to hurt yer feelings, but I must be honest. 'Tis the honor of a Highlander to always be truthful, but Lewis is no' being truthful at all. He's no' saying anything, and I wish he would."

Grif shouted, "Ysenda, if ye stop for a moment, then he might answer ye. Just for a wee moment. Seal yer lips, so I can find out if he likes ye too. Will ye court her, Lewis? Will ye? Is she no' the one ye are most interested in?"

"I wish to hear the answer to that question, Lewis, but I'm verra tired. Can I go to sleep now? Well, after ye answer. Then I'll sleep. But I could be pleased with yer answer or verra upset. Which is it? Do ye truly like me or do ye prefer Thea or Wenna? Who? Who?"

Lewis finally put his hand over her mouth and said, "'Tis ye, Ysenda. If I have eyes for anyone, 'tis ye. No' Thea or anyone else. Now close yer eyes and go to sleep."

"Suits me fine," she said, snuggling against him and closing her eyes. But she opened them a moment later. "I'm hungry. Are ye no' hungry, Lewis? Or should I just sleep?"

"Dinnae allow her to sleep," Maitland roared. "We're on Black Isle and a short distance from Matheson land. The firth is right there. In fact, I believe I hear a few horses headed our way. Isla probably sent her sire out to look for us."

"Horses! Could it be my sire? Or my mother?" She sat up to peer into the distance, but the area did not look familiar. "Oh look. Water! I love water. Mayhap we could go swimming on the morrow."

"'Tis a wee bit cold for a swim, lass. I dinnae think ye'd like it," Lewis said.

Maitland looked back at her. "Yer mother and father are on Ramsay land with yer grandparents and yer brother and sister. We're visiting yer aunt Brigid. Ye recall Aunt Brigid?"

First she scowled because she couldn't go swimming, but then she perked up listening to Maitland talk about her family. "Aye, I love Aunt Brigid. And Aunt Sorcha too. They are both so beautiful but so different. Aunt Brigid is dark-haired and Aunt Sorcha is blonde like me. Or nearly like me. Sometimes, my hair looks golden and sometimes light brown. Someone told me I looked like Grandda, but I dinnae wish to look like Grandda. Do ye no' think I look more like Aunt Sorcha? Will she be here? I'm so happy. But where is Mama?"

"Ye look like yer father and Aunt Sorcha, lass," Dyna said. "Those green eyes are the mark of being a grandbairn of Logan though."

"Everyone loves Grandda but sometimes he looks at me like I'm odd. I wonder why. Do ye know, Dyna? Or I'll ask Aunt Brigid. She'll know why." Her gaze went from one person to the next and then she stared out over the firth, the moon reflecting across the ripples in the water. "Is it windy?"

Dyna announced, "Hear me, all of ye. No discussing all her ramblings with everyone else. She's going to have enough trouble healing. Forget her musings when she's in her cups."

Grif said, "Fine. I'll agree. But ye'll be on Matheson land soon enough. 'Tis the finest oak tree ahead that marks the edge of their land. I would wager ye'll see someone from Matheson land soon enough, especially since Isla went ahead of us."

He'd no sooner finished his sentence when they came upon the oak tree, the sign they all knew indicated they were less than a quarter hour from the castle. Looking ahead, Lewis could make out movement. "Who is it, Maitland?"

The moonlight lit up the shapes of a few horsemen coming in their direction. She hoped they were Matheson guards at this hour. "Uncle Marcas? Or Shaw? Who is it?" Then she scowled. "I hope there are no bastard Englishmen here. I'm no' prepared to fight anyone."

Maitland couldn't hold his chuckle over that statement. "No English, lass," he called back to her. "Ye'll no' need yer bow." Maitland slowed his horse, waiting to see who was approaching.

Uncle Marcas, the Matheson chieftain,

approached and called out, "Grif, ye have my niece and she is hale?" His long dark hair blew in the wind coming across the firth, forcing him to turn his head just right so he could see clearly.

"See?" Ysenda pointed to the man in front. "Look at Uncle Marcas. His hair is blowing, so it is windy." She sat up to peruse the men behind Marcas, but she didn't recognize any of them. "No Mama or Da."

Grif had to shout to be heard. "Aye, she may have a broken leg, but she's safely wrapped up in a cart with Lewis tending her."

Marcas yelled, "Ysenda, are ye hale?" His horse came abreast of the cart.

"I'm wonderful, Uncle Marcas. How fare thee?" Her voice jumped up two octaves.

"What the hell? She's in her cups?" His gaze went from Ysenda sharply back to Maitland. "What did ye give her?"

"What did ye give me again?" she mumbled. "I canno' recall the name of that brew, but I surely liked it."

Maitland said, "The *breath of life*. 'Tis the only way we could get her here. Her leg is nearly in two pieces."

"And I like it, Uncle Marcas. Do ye? It burns my throat going down, but when it settles, it makes all my pain go away. All of it. Look I can lift my leg now. 'Tis no' broken anymore."

She did her best to show him, and Marcas whispered, "What is wrong with her, Lewis? 'Tis no' broken?"

"The other leg, Ysenda." He touched the

opposite leg for her, getting her attention because that leg hurt, not the other one.

"Of course! I forgot. Look, Uncle Marcas. This one really hurts. Will Aunt Brigid fix me?"

"Aunt Brigid and Tara will fix ye up just fine. They are waiting for ye. Isla told us of yer troubles. Dinnae worry." She thought she noticed a wide smile on her uncle's face. And everyone else's. They were all happy to be on Matheson land, just as she was.

"Good," she said, leaning back against Lewis and closing her eyes.

"No more *breath of life* for her, Maitland."

Maitland snorted.

Ysenda sat up and said, "But I like it. Dinnae blame Maitland."

Then she fell back and closed her eyes.

CHAPTER FIVE

LEWIS SAID, "DINNAE worry. She's still breathing fine. Allow her to rest before we arrive at Eddirdale Castle. If we're lucky, she'll sleep until after we get her inside."

Grif said, "And ye might need to plan a wedding, Chief."

Dyna blurted out, "A warning to ye, Grif. I know where ye are going with this. Leave it be."

But Lewis knew it was too late. Marcas had already heard.

"For whom?"

"Ysenda likes Lewis, and she just told him." Grif grinned from ear to ear after he said it, the kind of grin that made Lewis wish to grab him by the neck and shake him.

Maitland explained, "Ramblings of a young lass after her first taste of the *breath of life*, MacGriffin. Leave it be. She'll regret enough on the morrow."

Lewis said, "Many thanks, Maitland. She's no' herself. I will forget all she said."

Maitland explained, "Marcas, ignore him. He's taunting Lewis. She's happy because she is no longer in pain. An avalanche swept her and Lewis over the side of the ravine, but she was buried at the base. Lewis had to dig her out only to find her leg broken. It was no' easy getting her up the side, and she had to suffer through half the trip before I would give her a sip of the *breath of life.* 'Twas my judgment, no one else."

"My thanks for getting her here safely, all of ye. We'll talk later, Lewis," Marcas stated. "More important that we get her inside with this cold wind. Ye are sure her leg is broken?"

Lewis replied, "Aye. I felt the bone myself through the leggings. It needs to be repositioned, though I know naught of healing. I didnae attempt to do anything."

"Good. Allow my wife and her cousins to handle it. We have great healers here, as ye know," Marcas said. "Maitland, pull the cart straight up to the keep. The stable lads will follow ye. The rest of us will head to the stable."

Maitland did as he suggested, making his way along the edge once they were inside the wall, staying away from any of the stones in the courtyard. Ysenda slept like a wee bairn. Once there, Maitland dismounted, moving over to help Lewis remove the blanket so they could lift her out.

Maitland said, "Hand her to me."

Lewis refused. "I believe that movement will pain her enough to wake up. I can do it, but I ask ye to stand behind me so if I start to tip, ye'll straighten me back up. Then I'll be fine."

Marcas hollered to them, "I'll get her."

Lewis made his move to stand first so he

wouldn't have to hand her over to anyone. Ignoring a command from his chieftain was risky, but for some unknown reason, he could not just let Ysenda go. He was certain he understood her pain the best since he was the only one who saw exactly where the break was located in her leg. Therefore, he knew how to avoid the most painful spot better than anyone. Once he was standing and her leg had been settled without awakening her, he headed up the stairs to the keep.

Marcas said, "I see ye have her. Proceed with caution. I'll lead the way if ye follow him, Menzie."

The trio of men headed into the keep, across the great hall to a small chamber on the far side of the hall. Jennet and Tara were already inside awaiting them.

Isla rushed in behind them. "She is hale?"

Jennet led him to the back of the chamber and said, "Set her down on this bed. It is the sturdiest and with a broken leg, I dinnae want it moving at all."

Ysenda jerked awake when Lewis set her on the bed inside and declared, "Of course, I'm hale. And I'm happy too. Lewis said he was planning to court me if Aunt Brigid agrees. Where is she?" She glanced around the chamber, her gaze scanning slowly before she returned to everyone. "Greetings, all. I think I broke my leg when I fell down the ravine and all that snow fell on me. It buried me enough that Lewis had to dig me out."

All the faces turned to Lewis in shock. "She was buried?" Tara whispered. "For how long?"

Lewis nodded. "She was but not for long.

Fortunately, I landed next to her. Please ignore her ramblings," he spoke quietly. "We gave her a few sips of the *breath of life*. It made the journey easier." He made a quick move toward the door. "I have to take my leave, if ye all dinnae mind."

Lewis had the oddest feeling of the chamber spinning a bit. Maitland grabbed him by the arm and said, "Sit." He pulled a chair over and set him into it. "Ye look as though ye are about to fall over."

Lewis could feel his heart racing, though he did not understand why. And he had sudden pains in one leg whenever he stepped on it. His arm had been sore before but not his leg. "I dinnae feel so well, just happened after I came inside. I think I need some food."

"Tara," Maitland called over. "Once ye have checked Ysenda, Lewis has an arm injury that needs attention."

"Nay, dinnae worry about me. I'm fine. Just a meat pie or a hunk of bread will suit me."

Marcas' gaze narrowed as he watched him. "He's limping now. He wasnae before."

Maitland nodded. "I noticed. He was more worried about yer niece than himself."

"As any Highland guard should but still I'm pleased to see it in practice. I'll go for more help." Marcas left swiftly after eyeing Lewis carefully. "I'll see to the food and find Brigid. She needs to be here. Keep watch over him, Menzie. He doesnae look good."

"I'm fine, Chief," he insisted. There was nothing wrong with him that wouldn't be fixed with a good night's sleep. Then he peered up at Maitland. "I'm truly fine."

"Ye arenae fine. Ye took a hard fall down a ravine. For all we know, ye took a blow to the head. Ye would no' be the first to be fine for hours before yer injuries became apparent. Go lie on that pallet over there. Marcas will find ye some food, and I'll get ye a drink, but yer arm needs tending. Possibly yer leg. Ye are limping or have ye no' noticed? And can ye move all yer fingers?"

Lewis glanced down at both hands, unable to see them because he had not removed any of the coverings yet. He wiggled his leg and said, "I guess it does hurt some. I'm sure it will be fine on the morrow."

Maitland said, "I'll help ye remove yer mantle. The ladies will attend Ysenda. Ye need no' worry about her. Get yer mantle off and yer gloves so we can see yer arm. I dinnae like the looks of it." He lowered his voice. "Can ye move yer fingers? Ye arenae moving that arm, and the fingers look blue. Come with me."

Lewis followed Maitland, limping blindly, as he led him to the hearth at the end of the chamber. "Place yer hands closer, though no' too close. See if ye can start them moving again. I fear ye were forced to stay in one position for too long. Whether the cold or yer position, I know no', but we'll no' wait to find out."

Maitland touched his fingers, and Lewis reacted swiftly, pulling them back. They felt odd.

He didn't let Lewis go, instead reaching for his hands and tugging on them. "Unless ye'd like to lose them, allow me to assist ye. They are too gray. We must get them moving, get the blood pushing through again. When ye dinnae move yer hands in the cold, they stay that way." Maitland covered Lewis' hands with his own for a wee bit and then put them closer to the flames.

"I thought I moved them." He stared at Maitland, unable to comprehend exactly what was happening.

"Ye held Ysenda on yer lap and protected her from movement. To do that, ye had to keep yerself still and absorb all the cart gave ye. That kept yer arse moving and yer legs, but not yer fingers. They are beginning to loosen."

The door opened, and Brigid came in with a platter of food, a serving lass behind her with goblets of drink.

"Sit by the hearth," Maitland ordered before he called out to Brigid.

Lewis reached for a meat pie, picked it up off the platter, promptly dropped it, but Maitland was quicker. He caught it. "Give yerself a few moments to get yer fingers moving again."

Brigid took a goblet and handed it to Lewis. "Broth. Drink it. 'Twill warm ye from the inside out."

He did as she said, nodding his appreciation, but Maitland had to help him hold it. By the time he'd finished the broth, Brigid had gone to Ysenda's side. Maitland said, "Eat the meat pie. Ye'll feel better."

He picked it up gingerly, testing that he wasn't going to drop it, and then took a large bite, moaning with pleasure. "Aye, 'tis exactly what I needed."

All went well until he glanced over at Ysenda and noticed the healers doing their best to straighten her leg.

Lewis moved over to the pallet and settled on it. That was the last thing he recalled.

Ysenda woke up and had no idea where she was. Perhaps because her head pained her so much. Or was it her leg that hurt worse? She whimpered and tried to sit up, just to check herself over from head to toe and look around the chamber she was in, but she fell back quickly.

"Where am I?" Realizing she was talking to herself because no one else was there, she slowed her process and scanned the chamber again. "Is anyone there?"

A deep voice replied, "I'm here. Not far from ye and in about the same condition, Ysenda."

"Lewis?"

"Aye, 'tis me for certes."

He sounded odd, but then again, she had no idea what the hell was going on. Memories of the snowstorm began to piece together in her mind. Falling off her horse, being pelted with snow and rocks, falling over the edge of the ravine, landing on the bottom, and being buried in the snow. She had little memory after that.

"Lewis, ye saved me."

"I did have to dig ye out of the snow, but 'twas Maitland and Dyna who found the cart and pulled ye to Matheson land. I rode with ye. And now yer leg is broken."

"Nay…" She tested both, moving one with ease, but the other hurt terribly and felt like it was nailed to a board. A thought came to her and she had to ask for the truth. "Lewis. The animal. I heard it breathing next to me. What was it? A boar? A deer? Was it a big rabbit?"

He frowned, thinking for a moment. "Animal? I did no' see one in the ravine. Ye mean before we came through? I think I saw a deer then."

"Nay. One that was carried by the onslaught of rock and snow just like we were. When I was buried, there was an animal buried with me. I could hear it. I could *feel* its presence. What was it?"

"Ysenda, I did not see an animal near ye. There was nothing there. If it had been there breathing, I would have heard it. Besides, an animal has enough claws to dig its way out of snow. A boar's tusks could tear through the snow."

"Naught? Are ye sure? Mayhap he died in the avalanche. It could have been hit on the head or something similar. Something that took a few moments to kill its victim." She prayed Lewis would have seen something. Anything to convince herself that she was not losing her mind. That animal was there. She was certain.

He must have seen it.

"I'm sorry, lass, but I didn't see any animal. I walked all around the spot where ye were buried. I had to move around to get ye out. If there had been any living thing near ye, I would have seen it or felt it."

She'd lost her mind for certain. How had the animal gone from being part of her dream to being part of her life? She had not been asleep at all. It was no nightmare.

It had seemed as real as any creature standing near her.

"What happened to my leg? I dinnae remember. Everything is a wee bit fuzzy."

"They put something on yer leg to keep ye from moving it. Said 'twas the only way for it to heal correctly. Ye canno' walk for a fortnight. I only sprained mine, so I canno' walk for a few days. 'Tis why we are both here. And because this is where we get the magic brew, that liquid that is making yer mind fuzzy."

Ysenda had odd memories come back to her. Drinking some horrid potion that burned her throat but made her giddy at the same time. It also made her pain disappear. "I want more."

"More *breath of life*?"

"Aye, more of whatever Maitland gave me before. This hurts badly," she said, fighting the tears that threatened to drench her cheeks. She recalled the pain along the trip very well, but what she was experiencing now was far worse. Had someone wrenched her leg in ten different directions?

But she couldn't get the image of that beast out of her mind. She swore it was there. Could it be possible it had been there before they fell? Perhaps she had landed on it, knocking it out and it awakened a wee bit later. Had the beast bit into her leg? "Lewis, may I ask ye another question?"

"Of course."

"Are ye sure there was no animal anywhere near me? One with big teeth? It feels like something bit me in the leg." Was she losing her mind? She hated to repeat herself, but he must have forgotten something. It was there. She was certain.

"Nay, I didnae see one. The healers didnae mention a bite on yer leg. For certes they would have had they seen something suspicious. None of the horses fell over the edge, though one limped back with us. Did ye see a horse?"

"Nay. I just could no' recall what was real and what…" Her mind floated back to the odd memories.

"Lass, ye fell down a ravine. Probably hit yer head. It was snowing heavily and everyone was yelling. Brin and Ceit were nearly propelled over the edge too."

Lewis sounded so distant. She must have imagined it all. What he said made sense, but she knew better because this had been different.

This had been the first time she'd been faced with the beast when she was awake. All the other occurrences had been when she was asleep. It had appeared in a nightmare many times over the last few years, but never when she was awake.

Never.

She was surely going daft. At one point, she'd been excited about this patrol, had been thrilled to be included. She'd been in several battles already without any problems arising. But the snow, the avalanche, the fall, everything had changed her mind about this patrol. Would she be able to continue? Would she be a threat to everyone else?

Would her imagination make her see things in battle that weren't there? Could she risk endangering other lives?

"Ysenda? Are ye all right?" Lewis brought her back, away from fearsome dreams and evil creatures.

"I'm fine. Just some pain. And I'm verra tired too. Where is everyone?"

As if on cue, the door opened and footsteps came across to the back of the chamber where they were located.

"How are my two patients doing?" Aunt Brigid took a stool and sat next to her, fussing with her hair. "We had to fix yer bone, but I think 'tis verra straight now. Jennet did a lovely job. Ye are lucky. We feared it would go back crooked."

She had to ask the question foremost in her mind. "Was there anything unusual about my wound? Any teeth marks or anything odd?"

Aunt Brigid didn't mask her surprise. "Teeth marks? Nay. I saw naught like that. Were ye near an animal?"

She shook her head, trying to come up with a good reason for her strange questions. "Nay, it just…it hurts so much I thought it might be from more than just a broken bone."

Aunt Brigid leaned over to give her a soft hug. "Ysenda, ye have many bruises too. Ye look like ye've fought a score of Englishmen."

Lewis called out, "Ye bounced many times. More than I did, for certes."

"Do ye hurt much, Lewis?"Ysenda asked.

"Aye, I'm definitely sore in multiple places."

Sore was not the word she would use. "But it hurts badly, and I'm hungry. Have ye anything, Aunt Brigid? And I'm cold. How long must I stay here? Must I sleep here too?" Fear and confusion muddled her mind.

Broken leg? Multiple bruises? Couldn't walk? What was she to do?

Aunt Brigid took her hand and cocooned it inside her own. "Ye took a bad fall, but ye are lucky to be alive. Ye could have been buried and knocked over the head. So many things could have happened, but ye are here, and ye will heal. Ye willnae be able to walk on that leg for a fortnight at least. We will have to check on it. After this eve, we'll find a bedchamber for ye, so ye willnae have to use the stairs. We'll rearrange a wee bit, and ye'll have a chamber off the hall."

"No patrol? I canno' go home?"

"Nay. No riding a horse yet. I'm afraid ye will spend Yule with us, but I believe Isla has the right of it. I'm guessing yer mother and father will arrive with yer brother and sister, mayhap even Grandda and Grandmama. They said they may come here for the holidays, and knowing yer situation will surely bring them here. We'll have a fine holiday."

"But the patrol?" She'd wished to be part of the patrol for so long but now with all that had transpired, she would be pleased to step back for a bit. Perhaps it would give her mind the time it needed to stop with the nightmares.

"They havenae left yet, and they willnae for a bit. They are hoping Ceit and Brin arrive on the morrow or the next day. If no', they'll go back for them. The storm was enough to keep everyone here for another two days, at least. But we wish to move ye out and Lewis to a chamber above stairs for a few days before we send him out with the guards. We may have more people needing help on the morrow."

"That liquid. The brew I had when I was in the cart. Is there more? Where is Maitland? He may still have some. My leg hurts terribly, and my head hurts."

"Mine too," Lewis called out.

The door opened, and a serving lass entered with a trencher of stew and two bowls of broth thickened with barley and peas, setting all on the table along with some bread. "Need ye anything else, my lady?"

"Will ye fold the linens for me, Dolag?"

"Aye, right away."

Dolag tended to the task she was assigned while Aunt Brigid fussed with the food. "I wish ye to eat some broth, Ysenda. I'll help ye."

"I canno' eat stew or a meat pie. I think I would heave it up." Ysenda looked at the food and struggled to move. "And how can I eat lying down?"

Aunt Brigid said, "I'll help ye to sit in a moment. The stew is for Lewis. I'm sure he can eat it."

"Sure can." Lewis' voice warmed her a wee bit

every time he spoke. How she wished she could see him better. "Can ye no' hear the rumbling in my belly? Sounds much like a bear in the forest."

Ysenda couldn't help but smile at his banter. She was fond of him, more than she would admit to anyone.

Or had she already done so? Bits and pieces gathered in her mind, but then she shoved them away.

"Dolag," Aunt Brigid said to the lass. "When ye finish, give him the stew and half the bread for now. And a goblet of ale."

The serving lass took care of Lewis, but Ysenda was still flat on her back. "I canno' move with this contraption on my leg."

Isla came in and said, "I'll help ye, Aunt Brigid."

The two managed to get Ysenda propped up in the bed with pillows and her back against the wall, her leg rearranged on the end of the bed. "Here's the bowl of broth. It's thin, but I had cook put a few vegetables in it. Ye need something in yer belly before I'll give ye any more of that *breath of life*.

They set a flat board across her legs and set the bowl on it. "Go ahead and try it."

"It does smell wonderful. I am hungry. Many thanks to ye both for yer assistance. I dinnae like being so helpless." Ysenda took a sip of the broth and sighed. "'Tis still warm."

She reminded herself of how she felt just before they pulled her up the ravine in the sled contraption, that she'd be grateful for warm broth and a hearth. She was here and safe. That was something to be thankful for, so she enjoyed the broth and forced herself not to think on what the next few days would bring.

Aunt Brigid smiled and said, "I'll stay with ye for a bit more and then get ye settled for the night. I'm betting my dear brother will be here on the morrow. Whether Merewen comes with him or not, we'll see."

Ysenda wanted her mother. But she wasn't here, so Ysenda was forced to deal with what she had. She bent closer to her aunt and whispered, "Auntie, I have to pish. What do I do?"

"I'll help ye, dinnae worry."

She adored her aunt.

CHAPTER SIX

LEWIS WOKE UP in the middle of the night. He could hear Ysenda's breathing in her bed a short distance away from him. It was so dark in the chamber that he couldn't see her, but he knew her bed to be up against the wall so they could prop her up. His bed was in the middle of the chamber.

He relaxed to enjoy the moment and grinned. She was right. The *breath of life* they'd given him was quite fun. He had no pain at all at the moment. He wished she would wake up so he could share his thoughts with her.

He missed her. It sure as hell felt like he was indeed growing stronger feelings toward the lass. What that meant, he didn't know. But then again, he didn't care. He liked Ysenda. What more did he need to know than that?

"Ysenda?" He did his best to whisper, but it came out louder than he'd guessed. He didn't hear any change in her breathing. "Ysenda!"

He called again, this time coming out as a shout. He hoped no one was outside the chamber to overhear them. But, then again, perhaps he didn't care.

This *breath of life* had a way of making him not care about anything, and it was nice!

"What? Who said my name?" she asked.

Ysenda had heard him. He sat up, excited to have someone to talk with. "Me, Lewis. I'm right next to ye."

"What do ye want? I was sleeping." Her tone let him know she was a wee bit annoyed but not too much.

"Did ye drink all yer *breath of life*?" Lewis asked.

He hoped not. He could use a bit more, but only if she didn't need it. She deserved it after that awful injury she had. He'd nearly heaved watching her aunts fix it.

"Nay. I left a bit in the cup for the middle of the night. The pain is too much."

"'Tis the middle of the night. Ye can have it now."

"All right."

Her hand reached out to the small table next to her and grabbed the cup, swallowing a bit of the mixture. "Tastes so bad…"

"But?"

She giggled. "But then it tastes so good!"

"Can ye feel it still?"

"Aye. And it will be even better in a few moments. It takes the edge off this horrible pain. How is yer leg?"

"No' as bad as yers. Mine will heal faster. Do ye have any of that potion left?"

"A wee bit. But ye have to come and get it."
She giggled.

Mostly because her pain was disappearing
already he guessed, but he hoped she was giggling
because she liked him.

Lewis grabbed a stool and removed the blanket,
making sure his tunic was in place. Then, he took
his plaid and wrapped it loosely, enough to make
sure his bollocks were covered, if nothing else.
"I'm coming, lassie."

He slipped onto the stool and then managed to
find a way to slide the stool across the floor until
he was next to Ysenda.

"Greetings, lass," he said, wide-eyed. "Where is
that magical brew? Just a wee bit more will suit
me fine if ye dinnae need it."

She peered up at him and said, "Nae more for
me. Can ye help me sit up a wee bit, if ye please?"

Lewis threw the last of the amber gold down
his throat with a loud sigh. "Fine brew. My thanks
to ye. Here. I'll help ye up."

He fiddled and finagled until he had a pillow
propping her up. Her hair was a complete mess
but he did not care. She was still the prettiest lass
in all the land. Her light brown hair had a wee
wave to it and curled whenever she took it out
of her plait. There was a touch of gold in the
brown, unlike the red in his own. Her color was
more elegant and refined. And the green of her
eyes was quite regal, like an emerald glowing in
the middle of the night. A warm feeling spread
through him, something he knew came from the
brew, but he took a moment to enjoy it.

"How can ye be so pretty when ye've rolled down a ravine, been buried by an avalanche, and spent two hours in a cart?" he asked.

That giggle bubbled out of her cute little mouth, much louder than usual.

"Ye think I am pretty? Wait. Did ye no'? I'm trying to recall...did ye no' say ye would like to court me or something similar?"

"Did I? Could I? Would I have said such a thing to ye? I do recall something similar." He playfully echoed her words to tease her, and she responded with that playful scowl he knew so well. He stopped to pick up the flask of brew and took the last few drops in it.

She reacted instantly with a scowl. "I might have needed that."

He swallowed, leaned forward, and said, "Here, I'll give ye the last taste." And he kissed her, setting his lips against hers tentatively to see if she would respond to him at all.

She surely did.

Ysenda parted her lips with a sigh and threaded her fingers into his hair, something that caught him by surprise but was also pleasurable. He groaned with a carnality he hadn't expected. Her soft whimpers went straight to his member, especially when his tongue met hers, and she dueled with him as if they'd been together for years.

He leaned forward, doing his best to angle his head so he could delve deeper into her mouth, but he bumped his head against the bed. The motion caused her to squeal, and the two jerked apart.

"Och!" she shouted. "My leg. That hurt. Please be careful."

He rubbed his own shin, complaining as much as she had. "I hurt myself too. My pardon. I dinnae like this pain at all."

She moved. He moved. They bumped into each other again, and the two erupted in laughter.

Lewis fell off the stool.

That made Ysenda break into hysterics while Lewis did his best to figure out how to get back up with a sore arm and an injured leg. He pushed himself, moaning and groaning with each movement, but then fell back, enjoying her laughter so much that his own chuckles turned into guffaws, something he found he couldn't stop. And he found he didn't want to. Laughing with her was much more fun than being on patrol and wondering whether or not you were about to be attacked by the English.

Before they knew it, the two of them were laughing so hard they couldn't seem to end the episode. He managed to say, "I killed ye with my lips, did I?"

She mumbled between giggles, "Nay, yer kiss was so strong that it knocked us both over."

Then she laughed even harder.

He pushed himself back onto the stool. "Och, ye mean that we are so good together that we exploded with passion? That yer feelings for me are so strong that ye could no longer contain them?" He held his belly when his mirth overtook him again. He had tears ready to cover his cheeks, but he could not stop.

"Nay, because ye think I'm so pretty, ye were overcome with love. If ye ever ask me to marry ye, 'twill probably kill us both!" she drawled.

Her head tipped back with such a loud laugh that he could no longer speak.

Lewis said, "And if ye ever hear me tell ye that I love ye, then ye'll know something is definitely wrong." They both laughed at that one. "I'll be in trouble for sure if I tell ye that someday."

"For certes," she mumbled. "Especially considering my sire would never allow me to marry ye."

"Why? Am I too ugly?" He'd imbibed too much, but still, this comment caught him. What exactly did she mean by that? He had to ask.

"Because my sire always said I'd marry some laird or earl. Ye are neither."

Lewis forced himself to stand, then bowed to her. "Is this no' noble enough for ye? Shall I practice?" He reached for her hand and bent down to plant a kiss on it. "Would ye do me the honor of becoming my wife?"

The door opened, and there stood Marcas and Brigid. Marcas approached the two while Brigid fussed around the chamber. His voice called out to them in the dark, "What the hell are ye two doing?"

Brigid asked, "Did I hear ye two discussing marriage?"

Ysenda straightened a bit, but her voice couldn't shed all the laughter. "Only as a jest.

Ye see, Lewis managed to slide over here on the stool for another wee sip of the magic liquid, but then he fell off."

She smiled up at her aunt, unconcerned that they'd been caught in the middle of the night in a compromising position.

"Chief, I was helping her to sit up. We did naught wrong."

Marcas whispered to his wife, "Whose idea was it to leave these two alone in the healing chamber?"

"They are no' in an easy position to maneuver. Ysenda couldn't get out of bed if she wished to. We thought to let them sleep, so they'd be easier to move on the morrow. Plus we have to ready a chamber off the hall for Ysenda. She canno' climb the stairs."

He picked up the flask and took a sniff. "Who left this for them? Smells like a fine *breath of life* to me. Quite powerful. And 'tis empty now."

"I really like it, Uncle." Ysenda grinned. "Try it. Tastes mighty fine. Oh wait. Ye canno'. I drank it." A giggle bubbled up from her belly. "Is there no more?"

Lewis said, "I drank more than she did. She's fine. Dinnae worry about her."

He tried to sit up again, but promptly slid off his stool with a plop and fell backward with a yelp. That was enough to set Ysenda off again, laughing hysterically.

Marcas said, "Looks like we'll be spending the rest of the night here, Brigid. I wouldnae trust either one of them."

Brigid stared at Ysenda but then laughed herself. "I think they're both doing well, but I'll stay. Ye are correct. The brew has turned them both giddy. I'm sure their sense of judgment is totally compromised." She gave her husband a playful look. "After all they've been through, I canno' fault them."

Marcas replied, "Good point, but we canno' leave them alone. I would no' trust either of them."

Lewis sat up and attempted to slide back over toward Ysenda's bed.

Marcas barked, "Get yer arse over in that bed, Haggart!"

"Aye, Chief." Lewis did his best to stand up.

Pushing himself toward the bed, he took three limping steps and promptly began to tip over. Somehow, he managed to fall onto the bed just enough so he didn't hit his head.

His chieftain crossed his arms, shook his head, and then glared at his wife.

Brigid asked, "Ye dinnae recall when we were like them?"

"Nay," he started. "But I better get him into that bed before he breaks something else."

Lewis leaned his head back on the pillow, closed his eyes, and began to snore.

CHAPTER SEVEN

THREE DAYS LATER, Ysenda did her best to push herself up in her bed. It had been a chore to get her into her chamber with the contraption holding her leg still, but she'd made it with the help of Marcas, Grif, and Tevis. Ethan had come in and worked on her contraption, explaining to her that he was fixing something to help her move about on her own after she'd healed a few more days.

For that she would be eternally grateful. Even taking a pish was a chore. But Jennet and Ethan had shown her the chair they'd fashioned for others to use when they couldn't walk to the garderobe. A chair with a hole. Not at all lovely to look at, but it proved useful. She hated being dependent on someone else to move and empty the pot, but life had dealt her this, and she had to adjust.

Being alone in the chamber had given her plenty of time to think on her predicament. What the hell was she to do with her life? First there was the issue of patrol. Would she return when the time came? Memories of the avalanche still haunted her, especially the vision of the animal near her. She couldn't fathom how she'd thought there was one near her when there hadn't been one there at all. Surely, she was turning daft.

But why? And who could she dare ask about this issue? Surely not Maitland or any of her cousins. They'd all talk about it, and then her father would learn of her failure, and eventually her grandmother and grandfather would hear of it.

What would they say to her?

The other issue she had was concerning Lewis. What exactly had they discussed? She smiled every time she recalled their various episodes of laughter the other night, especially when poor Lewis had fallen off the stool. They'd both had too much of the *breath of life*, and her headache the next day convinced her of it. Why did the two seem to go together?

But what bothered her most was they had jested about courting and marrying. He'd kissed her and she'd kissed him back, something she was unlikely to forget anytime soon. But he'd teased her about saying he loved her. In fact, if her memory served her right, he'd said if he ever told her he loved her, it would mean he was in trouble.

In other words, Lewis loving Ysenda was a complete jest to him. At times, she'd had a brief wish that they could have a relationship together, one that wasn't always banter, but one that involved caring for each other, talking about their problems, discussing a future they could have together. He'd kissed her with more passion than any other lad had ever done and she'd liked it.

No, she'd loved it. The truth was she was falling for Lewis, and he thought their relationship to be a jest. She recalled the pain his comment had caused, even when half in her cups. And then she'd told him an outright lie about her sire insisting she marry a nobleman.

While he'd never said such a thing, they'd never discussed who she should marry. Would they be fussy? Would they insist on someone with nobility in their blood? Her mother didn't see things that way, but what about her father and grandfather?

She felt a wee bit of guilt over that lie, but she had to retaliate with something after he'd insulted her with his jest comment.

The true question was, why wouldn't he consider her suitable to be his wife?

She'd always known she wasn't beautiful like Aunt Sorcha or Aunt Brigid, that Ceit was the prettiest of the lasses on patrol. But she never thought of herself as someone who couldn't attract a man.

Clearly, she couldn't. She forced that thought from her mind and returned to all the happenings at Eddirdale Castle. If someone would just visit her, she might hear something interesting.

Though she did not wish to see Lewis. If she did, she'd be inclined to slap him for his rude comment. There was something wrong with him, but it wasn't because he was falling in love with her. The daft brute could fall for Thea or Wenna, and she'd not care at all.

Perhaps she'd fall for Willum.

Things had been busy for the healers, or so she'd been told. There had been some kind of animal attack on the guards, so there had been two or three in the healing chamber for that. Ceit and Brin had returned, but they'd both left already, along with the rest of the patrol. Ceit had gone first while Brin had stayed back, but he'd changed his mind and disappeared not long after. They said it would be a short journey because all would be going home for Yule, so Tevis would return and update them all on what was going on in the land of the Scots.

She and Lewis were off patrol until the new year came along.

She hadn't seen Lewis since she moved into this chamber, but mostly because she didn't see anyone but those who stopped in. Somehow, she was quite certain her uncle had forbidden Lewis or any other man from stepping inside her bedchamber. And how was she to leave and speak to anyone? Jennet had given her a metal bell to clang if she needed anything, but she hated to bother anyone.

She had never been the type of person to be saddened by her situation, but it was beginning to sink its tendrils deep into her belly.

The door opened, and Isla flew in. "Straighten up. Yer sire is her with yer grandda."

"Da and Grandda? Grandda is traveling in the snow that quickly? I thought they would wait until the weather had improved." She couldn't have been more shocked. The possibility of their arrival had been mentioned to her, but she hadn't expected any of them for another sennight.

Grandda was getting up in age where he rarely traveled unless it was of vital importance.

Isla threw a comb at her. "Fix yer hair. Ye are a sight, lass. Allow me to find a tunic ye can wear. Something clean. Ye still have blood on those leggings."

"They're the only ones that will stretch. The wool ones are too tight and itchy."

"Mayhap if ye are fortunate, Grandmama sent some new ones along. She often sends them to Aunt Brigid. And if so, I want a pair too. She makes the finest." Isla flew around the chamber, fixing it the best she could.

"Nay, she doesnae."

Isla stopped fussing and stood up straight. "Whose are better than Grandmama's?"

"Wenna's. Ye should see how Aunt Maggie makes them. They have a soft nap to them. She makes them from animal skins, and they are warm and so soft."

"Then I wish for a pair of those too, especially for winter patrol."

A knock sounded at the door just before it flew open, but Isla caught it before it hit the wall. "Uncle Logan, Aunt Brigid says to stop breaking the doors."

Her grandfather strode in with a sheepish grin. "Och, ye are correct. I'll try to remember. Now where is the invalid?"

Her father pushed past her grandfather and moved right over to the bed, stopping to stare at her leg. "Ah, lass. It doesnae look good. I would wager 'twas a painful fall and a long journey here."

Surprised that tears erupted so quickly, she reached for her father, and he sat on the bed next to her, wrapping her in his arms. "Mama and Grandmama will be here in another couple of days. Ye know our chieftain. He has to send a score of guards or more, and they both plan to stay for Yule. And Grandmama wished to wait for the snow to melt some. Ye know how she is in the cold."

"Truly? Ye dinnae mind?" she whispered. "Yule? Ye'll stay for Yule? Grandda, ye willnae leave before then?" She had a sudden need for all of her family to be around for the holiday.

Grandsire said, "Nay, I promised Brigid we'd visit soon. We'd been thinking of coming, but this forced our hand to commit to it. Yer siblings will be along too. We were trying to convince Brenna to come, but she doesnae travel much of late, so dinnae expect her. We'll have a fine Yule. Now, come out to the hall and tell us all about the avalanche. I need to get something to eat." He turned away and waved at her, as if she could follow easily.

"How can I get there, Grandda? If ye havenae noticed, I canno' walk." She hated to be so sarcastic, but what the hell was he thinking? "I have been in this chamber ever since I left the healing room. I'm stuck."

"Why do ye think I brought yer sire along?"

He turned back and waved at her father, who shrugged his large shoulders.

The man she adored more than any other reached down and scooped her up, her squeal loud enough to make her grandfather turn around.

"Da, balance the contraption for me, would ye?" Her father glared at his sire. "Ye cannae let her leg just fly around."

"Dinnae give me that look, Gavin. Ye only need to ask," Grandda said.

The two maneuvered her through the door, and her father led her over to a chair near the hearth.

Aunt Brigid said, "Wait before ye settle her. I wish to prop her leg."

Tara joined her aunt, and together, they settled her quite nicely in front of a warm fire. She shivered with delight as the heat coursed through her. "Finally, I am warm."

The two women fussed over her with blankets and sent for a goblet of vegetable broth for her. When they finally left her alone, she looked up, surprised to see Lewis directly across from her in another chair with his leg also propped up.

"Lewis," she offered. "How do ye fare?"

She tried to forget their antics in the healing chamber but then recalled their kiss. Her blush came instantly.

"Better than ye, I see. How is yer pain?" He looked handsome as ever, that finely chiseled jaw of his reflected in the flames of the fire. But every time she looked at him, a different memory popped in her head, one she didn't like. How had they gotten so deep in their cups?

How foolish had they been? She had a vague feeling she needed to be embarrassed about something but couldn't recall exactly what. Perhaps it would be best if she didn't banter with the man any longer. After all, their relationship was a jest to him.

Isla, Grif, and Isla's sister, Charlotte, came down the stairs to join them. "Greetings, Uncle Logan, Gavin." Logan was Isla and Charlotte's great uncle.

Grif said, "Nice to see ye two are out of yer chambers and among the living here, Lewis and Ysenda. We feared they'd never let ye out."

Lots of jests, jokes, and greetings all around took place while the serving lasses brought porridge, baked apples, and bread enough for all and set them on the sideboard.

Her father stood and asked, "Yer choice, Ysenda?"

"I'll have a bowl of porridge with some honey, if ye please."

He brought her a bowl and some goat's milk and set it on the table next to her. She frowned, glancing at the goat's milk, something she didn't drink often.

Aunt Brigid said, "Ye better drink it. No more special potion for ye."

"Why no'? It helped with my pain," she argued.

Visions of Lewis laughing on the floor in the healing chamber popped into her head, along with Marcas and Brigid standing over him. Probably better not to ask about it.

"I have another potion for ye to try. I'll go find it," Aunt Brigid said.

Begrudgingly, she picked up the goat's milk and downed half of it, since she found it more refreshing than she expected. She turned her attention to the porridge.

Her father and grandfather sat at a nearby table enjoying the baked apples and bread. It was a nice, quiet moment until it was ruined.

Charlotte, Isla's younger sister who spoke her mind, asked, "'Tis true ye and Lewis are going to marry, Ysenda?"

Ysenda had just taken a bit of her porridge and nearly spit it out.

Lewis choked on a bite of something he'd been chewing.

"Nay!" Ysenda shouted. Someone had to deny the ridiculous comment while Lewis was choking. "'Tis a most ridiculous notion, Charlotte. Please dinnae repeat it."

Charlotte moved over to stand in front of her and explained, "But I heard people talking about it. Why would they talk of it if it werenae true?"

"Who?" she demanded, a little too harshly. "Who was talking about it? And what exactly did they say? I need to know because none of it is true."

She had to put a stop to this before it went too far.

Charlotte continued, "Grif and Willum said ye liked each other. Dyna said it was the brew.

Maitland said it was true but to be quiet about it. And Aunt Brigid said that she heard ye two talking of marriage."

"Marriage?" her sire bolted from his seat. "Explain, daughter."

She had no idea what her father's response would be to Lewis as a suitor, but since Lewis wasn't interested in her, why even suggest it? Lewis could fall down the ravine again for all she cared.

"We didnae discuss marriage. Where do people come up with such ideas? Da, I'm no' ready to marry anyone, and if I were, it surely would no' be Lewis." Her chin jutted up a notch as if to convince everyone she was telling the truth.

Even if it was a lie.

"And if I were to marry, it surely would no' be ye either, Ysenda," Lewis grumbled.

That comment was so true that it hurt. While they didn't have to be in a relationship, he need not insult her so easily.

Even if she'd insulted him first.

What the hell was happening to her? Her life had been totally upended because of an avalanche.

She had to admit that if she were asked, Lewis would be the first one she'd choose if she were to marry. But she was not even considering such a thing since he'd considered their relationship a jest. She ignored his insult, vowing not to let his rejection bother her either. But why would he *surely* never marry her?

Aunt Brigid asked, "Are ye forgetting all the *breath of life* ye had, lass?"

"*Breath of life!*" her father bellowed. "Who gave her that? She's too young. Are ye all daft on Black Isle?"

"Maitland did. He had to do something to get her here, Gavin," Aunt Brigid explained. "If ye'd seen her leg before Tara, Jennet, and I straightened it, ye'd no' be asking us that."

"What the hell happened exactly? I wish to hear it now from my daughter's lips." Her father crossed his arms and waited. The entire hall was silent.

Ysenda said, "I'll explain, Da. The blizzard started before we crossed the ravine, but it hadn't been snowing for long, and Dyna and Maitland thought we could make it across before the snow was too deep. We'd have been held up for days had we not crossed."

"And stuck in a cave for the night like Brin and Ceit," Lewis added.

Ysenda continued, "When we came across, an avalanche hit Lewis and me, knocking us over the edge. In the process, I bounced a few times, and when I landed, I was buried in the snow." Her lip began to tremble as she thought on the frightening event. She was lucky to be alive and she knew it. Opening her eyes to know she was buried in snow was one of the worst moments of her life, especially when she'd thought she was about to be attacked by some invisible beast.

Isla said, "I'll take over for ye, Ysenda. I was there too. None of the horses went over the edge, strangely enough. Ceit and Brin were at the end and had to spend the night in the cave because the path was blocked. Maitland was able to speak with Lewis, and he confirmed that Ysenda was buried but he could see her. Once he got her out, he told Maitland he thought her leg was broken. Maitland and Dyna sent some of us on to Matheson land for help while they went in search of a cart, leaving Grif and Willum at the end of the ravine to watch over them and the horses."

"I couldnae see anything, Grandda. Lewis saved me," she said, tears now rolling down her cheeks. "'Twas a horrible thing to open yer eyes and only see darkness. I thought I was going to die. To feel the weight of the snow everywhere and ice digging into yer cheeks. And it was a cold, eerie darkness." She hated that her voice had risen to a pitch she never used, but she was unable to stop herself, the fear of death and the unknown beast now fresh in her mind.

"Ye dug her out, Lewis?" Grandsire asked in that quiet tone she rarely heard from him. "How did ye find her?"

"Her voice, I think. I yelled for her, and I could hear her mumbling or something. I did what anyone would do." Lewis glanced at her, but then stared at his hands. "I took my hand coverings off and dug as fast as I could."

Grif said, "By the time Maitland returned, besides freeing her, Lewis had also built a contraption to set her on and managed to get Ysenda on it. He'd pulled her to the end of the ravine and we were able to help get her to the top, but only because of the contraption he made. 'Twould have been nearly impossible without it."

Everyone turned to stare at Lewis.

Grif paused, then said, "We got her into the cart, and Maitland pulled her as carefully as he could." Then he glanced over at Ysenda. "But the poor lass was in terrible pain."

Lewis hopped out of his chair on one leg and declared, "Aye, she was. More than most people would be able to bear. When Maitland said he had a flask of the *breath of life* from a friend, we all insisted he give it to her. She was in too much pain. I could no' bear…"

Ysenda forced herself to stop the tears, but all the memories of the pain, the ride in the cart, the fear of not surviving all coursed through her. "Da. It hurt so bad, and Lewis insisted he'd ride in the cart with me, but only if Maitland gave me some of the brew. I didnae know what it was, but I took a sip. I still feared I was going to die on the way to Black Isle. 'Struth is I've never experienced such pain before." She rubbed both her eyes and stared up at her sire. "But it did make the rest of the trip more bearable. What would ye have had me do?"

Lewis stood and said, "It was a horrible experience for all of us. I'll leave ye alone to discuss it, but we did the best that we could with a difficult situation. Ye should no' be blaming anyone for anything. And there was no discussion of marriage." He did his best to leave the keep, limping all the way.

Her father strode over and kissed her forehead after Lewis left. "I understand. I'll no' be angry with ye. But tell me true. Did anything else happen between the two of ye that I should know? Have ye been compromised by anyone during this ordeal?"

Aunt Brigid shouted, "Gavin, hellfire but nay! Stop acting like Lewis did something wrong. They were with Maitland and Dyna, and then they were here with me and Marcas. They both had some of the potion because his leg and arm were both sprained, and her leg was broken and had to be set straight by three of us. Leave the man alone, and for heaven's sake, stop pestering yer daughter. She's been through enough. This is my home and she's under my care. Leave her be."

Uncle Logan, who had kept quiet through much of it, said, "I agree with yer sister, Gavin. Let Ysenda be. Yer daughter was on patrol and took a severe injury. The *breath of life* was warranted. If she was in her cups because of it, 'tis fine. Too much could kill her, but Maitland judged it correctly. And I'm sure Brigid kept a close eye on her once she arrived here. We can be grateful they were close enough to come here where there are skilled healers."

Her sire pursed his lips, and he moved back toward the table. "Fine, I'll agree to leave the issue be once I hear from her lips that she was no' compromised by anyone. Ysenda?" His fists settled on his hips, and he turned back to his daughter.

She closed her eyes and said, "Nay, Da. I was in my cups. We jested and laughed, but I wasnae compromised by Lewis or anyone else. And we are no' getting married."

She neglected to tell him the truth because it

would cause nothing but trouble, but the truth was, she couldn't recall all of what was said between the two of them.

But she surely did recall that kiss.

And it was one delicious kiss.

CHAPTER EIGHT

L EWIS NEARLY FELL until he found a
bench to sit on but only because his hopping
skills had definitely improved. The crisp air
suited him just fine. He had to get away from
the inquisition that was going on inside the hall
with Ysenda and her family.

Grif followed him out the door. "Getting too
intense in there for ye?"

"Aye," he replied, glancing over his shoulder to
see if anyone else had exited with Grif. "Ysenda
and I were clearly both in our cups and jesting.
Why is everyone taking it so seriously?"

Grif sat on the bench. "Because ye are talking
about her father and grandfather. Logan Ramsay
especially has quite a reputation for being difficult.
He was a spy for the Scottish Crown for years, so
he knows many people. I imagine he's got an idea
about who he wishes each of his granddaughters
to marry. But I believe he would accept ye as a
suitor."

"He need no' worry about it. I'm no' interested."
His reply came out a bit more harshly than he'd
intended, but Ysenda had declared she'd never

consider marrying him. He had to admit the comment stung, even if she was mimicking his own comments about not choosing her.

How had an avalanche brought him to this situation?

"Ye are lying. Ye forget I know ye well enough to have seen ye around many lasses. Ye are interested in Ysenda. Now I'm going to the stable to take care of my horse. Think on it for a bit. Dinnae let an old Highlander scare ye away from pursuing a lass ye have feelings for. In my opinion, ye make a good match. She could make ye verra happy."

Grif took his leave and he had to admit the man was right. Except for one thing. Having a serious relationship with Ysenda would probably not make him happy at all. Continuing to pursue Ysenda would bring even more scrutiny, and his secret would be uncovered for sure. He'd rather not pursue her than to fall for her and be rejected.

It would be simpler if he stayed away from her now. Then he had another odd thought. Perhaps it was time to visit his father and his sisters, see if anything had changed about their past.

His past.

Perhaps he shouldn't have walked out, but the questions were too difficult. He wanted to leave before he was asked a question he didn't wish to answer. He and Ysenda had shared a life-changing experience, one neither of them would ever forget. An experience that had damaged them both.

But they hadn't done anything wrong. They'd

shared a kiss, and that was it. Nothing anyone needed to be upset about.

But the less her father and grandfather knew, the better.

The banter of the guards caught him, and he had the odd feeling that he wished he was just a Matheson guard. Being on patrol, having to answer to all the Ramsays and the Grants was proving more than he'd bargained for. He hadn't given the issue much thought until he was confronted by it as he was now. As a guard, he only had to worry about what the second man in charge thought of him. He didn't have to deal with the chieftain of the clan or any of the wives. How was one to deal with those kinds of people?

He guessed they didn't spend all their time shouting at each other the way his father yelled at everyone under his roof.

Gavin and Logan Ramsay had never even noticed him before. Now he was subjected to intense scrutiny. All because of the possibility of a relationship with Ysenda.

Everything was taking on a different perspective, even patrolling with a beautiful lass like Ysenda. Oh, he'd joked about courting her, jested about marriage, but the truth was that he knew it could never be. If anyone seriously considered him as a suitor for Ysenda, they would definitely start asking questions. He knew this in his heart, yet he hadn't considered that there could be repercussions from just befriending the lass. Even that could bring up multiple questions.

Where was his family? Where did they live?

And the most threatening question of all: Why did his small family leave Clan Ross?

No one knew the answer to that question but his sire and the chieftain of Clan Ross. And he had no desire to reveal the truth of the matter. If Ysenda ever learned the truth of why he'd come to Matheson land, she'd never have another thing to do with him. As far as he knew, no one knew the truth. Not even Grif. He'd managed to keep it hidden thus far, and he had to make sure it stayed that way.

And if her parents learned the truth, they'd forbid her from having anything to do with him. He'd probably never be allowed to speak to her again. How he wished he could right this wrong. It was utterly unfair, but there was nothing he could do about it.

Perhaps he needed to face up to this travesty again. Since he had time before the patrol would depart again, perhaps it was time to go home and find out if there was anything else he needed to know about that fateful event. Had anything new ever been discovered? To find out, he'd have to visit with his father and his sisters again. As soon as he could dismount a horse without injuring himself worse, he'd go look them up.

It was probably going to be a good idea to get away from Clan Matheson for a wee bit anyway.

The door opened, and the sound of footsteps carried across the stone courtyard. Ysenda's father strode straight toward him. He was a large man, taller than Logan with the same size shoulders. His light brown hair fell to his shoulders, and he hadn't lost a bit of it like many men as they aged.

"Lewis, may I join ye?" Gavin asked.

"Aye, my lord."

"Nay, not my lord. Gavin Ramsay to ye, and I'm pleased to make yer acquaintance."

That statement unsettled him, but he vowed to listen and be polite. "Gavin."

"I offer my gratitude for saving Ysenda's life. Tongues wag, and rumors gain wings, so I knew I had to come and see for myself exactly how my daughter fared and hear what happened from her lips. I had no idea she had been buried in the snow. I thank ye for being vigilant and persistent. It could have ended verra differently."

"Ye would have done the same, so there is nae reason to thank me. It was a frightening event for both of us." That was an honest reply. The man was actually treating him with respect over the matter. He guessed he deserved it. After all, he could have deserted her many times on the trek from the bottom of the ravine to Matheson land.

"My sister seems to think that there is something between ye and Ysenda. Is there?" Gavin's eyes bore into his, something Lewis didn't like. It was as if her father could see inside Lewis, uncover what he was hiding, though he knew it was impossible. But the dampness on the palms of his hands told him otherwise. It was winter, the air was freezing, and the sweat on his hands could clean a trestle table after twenty guards ate there.

"Nay. Ysenda and I are friends. We tease each other when we are on the road, probably because we have a similar sense of humor."

"Och, ye are sarcastic like Ysenda?" Gavin crossed his arms and Lewis caught a gleam in his eye that reminded him of Ysenda. Did she get her sense of humor from her father?

Lewis smiled. "Aye. I like her sense of humor. She's not serious all the time like some of the others. I like to break the tension on patrol. 'Tis too difficult otherwise."

Gavin assessed him, his gaze traveling from his head to his toes, and then up to the gray skies of winter in the Highlands. He said nothing, and Lewis had no idea what he was thinking.

Lewis said, "Honestly, we were both in our cups from the *breath of life*. It made us laugh harder than I have ever laughed. We may have forgotten some of our problems and a bit of our inhibitions. We jested more than ever, but I never forgot who Ysenda was, that she is someone who always deserves my respect."

Gavin nodded and then said, "Obviously or ye would no' have fought to get her out of the snow and across the ravine. Nor would ye have protected her in the cart in a valiant move to end her pain. Many thanks to ye, Lewis. Is yer sire a guard here?"

"Nay, he is no'. He lives in a village a distance away. I lost my mother many years ago."

"I'm pleased ye are no' interested in her. I have a husband in mind for her when she finishes patrol. I wish to see my daughter happily matched and living on Ramsay land. Not here on Matheson land where I'll rarely see her. Again, many thanks for taking care of her. I'm going to return to my daughter. If ye need anything at all, please let me know." Gavin gave him a quick nod and turned on his heel to head back to the keep.

Lewis nearly let a question slip, but he reined the temptation in. What would the man say if he knew the truth about him? Would any of the famous Ramsay contingency support Ysenda marrying a man who'd been forced to leave Clan Ross?

He had serious doubts about it.

Gavin had only been gone for about a quarter of the hour when a guard approached him from the stable, one of the new young guards they'd hired after he and Grif had joined the patrol.

"Is the pretty blonde with the broken leg still inside?" The fool had a grin on his face that Lewis didn't like. The truth was he had the urge to put his fist in the middle of that grin, but he quashed it.

"Who are ye?" He had no idea what the lad's name was, but he was too young for Ysenda.

"Duncan. I'm going to grab a meat pie, and I heard the lovely lass is finally in the hall. I wish to meet her."

The brown-haired guard was tall and thin, a wide smile full of white teeth filling his face. The hope in Duncan's gaze was something Lewis hadn't seen in a while. How did one destroy someone's hopes? With a quick fist in his face? Or should he tell him the truth about Ysenda's family? Then he decided the lad needed to find out for himself.

"Why? Ye need a reason to speak with her." He

really didn't but Duncan didn't need to know that.

"Because I'd like to meet her. She's a beauty. Why else would I wish to go?" Duncan gave him a crooked grin and smirked.

"She's no' available. Only to noblemen." He did his best to stare the lad down, but his glare didn't seem to affect the boy at all. And he was still a boy.

"Is she inside? Is she hale?"

"She's hale, but she's busy."

Duncan frowned but then his face lit up. "I'll see for myself." He took off for the keep, tripping on the first step but catching himself with a chuckle.

Lewis would have chased after him to make sure he kept his distance from her, but since he was dependent on hopping, he decided to stay where he was for a few moments. He wasn't ready to go back and confront the Ramsay men.

Let them see how they liked Duncan.

But what if they did? "Hellfire," he muttered to no one in particular. Hellfire if he had to admit to himself that he didn't wish for anyone to touch Ysenda.

Duncan disappeared inside the keep. No sooner had he gone inside, then Grif came from the stable, headed his way. "Ye are hale? Ye need help moving back inside?"

"Nay, I'm fine out here. 'Tis nice to get a breath of fresh air after being cooped up inside the last few days. And I dinnae even know how many days it has been." He sighed, repositioning his leg to try to minimize the ache that wouldn't leave him. Then he noticed something else. Grif had an odd expression on his face, as if he was doing his best to contain his laughter.

A sudden insight into his friend's odd behavior occurred to him. Grif could be sneaky when he wished to be, though he knew his friend would not hide anything if confronted. Lewis said, "Ye know Duncan. Did ye send him along?"

Grif chuckled. "Nay, he's one of many talking about Ysenda's good looks and how difficult this must be for her. I did suggest he speak to ye before he ventured inside. I take it he did. Nothing was going to stop that lad from chasing after the pretty blonde. I thought it best to let ye know what he was about. For Ysenda's sake, not yers."

Lewis bolted off the bench, only to fall back down again when the pain ripped through him. "Hellfire." A loud groan erupted from him because he was sick of dealing with the pain whenever he moved, but he reminded himself that Ysenda's pain was far worse than his. "Tell them all that she's unavailable."

Grif arched a brow at his friend, then crossed his arms. "Truly? And why is that?"

He wouldn't give him the answer that sat deep in his soul, that Ysenda belonged with him. Instead he replied, "Because her father has someone in mind for her."

"Not ye?" He caught Grif's expression change. It was no longer one of glee but one of surprise.

"Nay."

Grif murmured, "My apologies for that

inquisition. The Ramsays are good people, but ye'll learn that if ye set yer sights for one of the daughters, ye'll be tested many times. Could be the man is testing ye now."

"I havenae set my sights on anyone, Grif. Why is everyone acting strangely about this? Telling tales?" He didn't wish to cause Ysenda any embarrassment from anything he'd done, though he wished his memory would serve him better. "She was in her cups on the way back from the ravine. And I agree with Maitland that it should no' be discussed. Leave it be for now."

"I agree. She was in her cups, and ye both had been through a terrible ordeal."

"As we all had. No need to repeat foolish comments made under unusual circumstances, is there?" He wished this whole conversation to end.

"Just between ye and me, I think she is interested in ye, Lewis. I think ye could make a fine pair. Do ye no' have any interest in the lass? Because if ye do, now would be the time to act on it." This time, his friend was as serious as he'd ever seen him. Did he truly think Lewis had a chance with Ysenda? Then he shook his head, memories of Gavin Ramsay's words about having chosen a match for her bouncing in his mind.

He shrugged his shoulders, unsure of how to answer. Perhaps it was time to be honest with Grif about his past. Rubbing his hand across the scruff of his unshaven cheek, he said, "I like Ysenda, but I have no noble blood in me, as ye know. I'm no' going to chase after Logan

Ramsay's granddaughter. If she is interested in me, then I hope she'll let me know, but I think all her comments came from what she ingested. She was having fun. 'Tis how I look at it. We often tease each other. Ye know how we banter. I'm no' going to take it any other way. Two friends in their cups."

"So ye were no' discussing marriage?"

He couldn't recall exactly what they had talked about, but if they had, it had been in jest. "I suppose it could be possible. We had quite a bit of the brew in the healing chamber. What I recall was how hard we laughed about whatever we were discussing, so if marriage came up, we were no' being serious about it. It had to have been in jest. I'd prefer no' to discuss it anymore, Grif."

Grif nodded and clasped his shoulder. "The only other thing I'll say is that I am proof that noble blood doesnae matter. If I can marry a Ramsay, so can ye. Please get that out of yer head."

"I understand what ye are saying, but yer history is no' the same as mine."

Grif looked at him with a puzzled expression. "What are ye referring to? I know no' much about ye before ye came here."

"And ye never will hear it all. No one will."

That ended the discussion. Grif got up and helped him back inside. He probably shouldn't have been so short with one of his closest friends, but he knew one thing for certain.

Even Grif wouldn't understand the truth.

CHAPTER NINE

YSENDA SAT IN the hall, watching the morning activity. There was a part of her that was ready to go out on patrol any time soon, but the ache in her leg reminded her that she'd not be going anywhere.

But would she truly like to go?

She'd so enjoyed going on the patrol when she'd been invited by Maitland and Dyna. The camaraderie among the female archers was something she enjoyed. They spoke of the challenges and any failings they believed they had, discussing how to improve their aim and their shots. Being involved in the battles against the English had brought her into a whole new world, an exciting world.

She loved patrolling and scouting in search of the English who marauded her land. She took satisfaction in each arrow that met its mark, felling the bastards as they approached her comrades. And from her perch in the trees, she had come to love to see the backs of her enemies as they retreated from the Scottish defense.

But the weather had been summer and early

autumn, there had been no nasty dreams of beasts, and there had been no travel restrictions.

No blizzard, no ice, no breathing boars, no avalanche, no unmanageable pain.

She wondered if she would ever get past this challenge. Would she ever be able to return to patrol with no restrictions? No fears? She had to believe the time would come. Her leg would heal, the snow would disappear...if only the beast would do the same.

Ysenda finished her porridge when Isla came up and took a seat next to her. "Are ye no' bored yet?"

"I feel as though I am slowly losing my mind. But what choice do I have?" She glanced up at her cousin, a sudden feeling of gratefulness surging through her. Isla had been forever faithful, checking in on her often.

"I think ye could have two choices this morn. Many of us are going in to make sweet treats for the holiday. And I overheard there is to be a big training session in the lists. Ye know how it goes. Grandsire is challenging all the guards to meet him in the lists. They will all be there."

"But I cannae do anything. Why would I go there?" She'd prefer to be on the archery field practicing, but she'd been forbidden by her father to even think on it.

Isla let out a very unladylike snort. "I know I'd prefer to be watching all those men work their muscles than to have my hands in various jellies and pastries. I think I overheard yer sire say he was going to meet Grandda there. He'll take ye out. I stepped out and the sun is actually warming the day. What say ye?"

Her sire came up behind them. "What are ye two planning?"

"Da, would ye take me out this morn? Isla said there's a challenge in the lists. And she said the sun is out. Can I no' get some fresh air? Watch the challenges?" She peered up at him, hoping he'd agree.

"I think 'tis a fine idea. Are ye ready, lass? Because I'm about to head there now."

She pointed to the peg on the door. "If ye get me my mantle, please? I'll take an extra plaid for my feet."

Isla said, "If ye go near the coastline, Uncle Gavin, ye'll see two large boulders that are quite comfortable. And there's a bench there too. That way she can breathe in the fresh air coming across the bay. 'Tis in the sun in the morn. Ye can see all the lists from there."

Her sire stepped over to the peg and found her mantle, and Isla helped her don the warm wool garment, taking care to guard her leg. "I'll get dressed and follow ye out, help ye maneuver yer leg in that contraption."

"My thanks to ye, Isla." Her spirits suddenly brightened for the day. Just the idea of breathing in fresh air and soaking up the sun sounded heavenly to her.

A short time later, the two had her arranged on the bench. The view was stunning as she watched the few boats on the water from one side and the men practicing in the lists outside the curtain wall of the castle from the other side. There had to be more than a score there already, though their shapes blended in together.

Until she saw one man in particular—Lewis.

Her gaze fell on him as he parried with her father, her grandsire watching from the side, shouting various thoughts out as they worked. She could tell he was favoring his one arm, but he was still fighting hard. Unable to hear his words, she really wasn't the least bit concerned because watching Lewis was like watching a well choreographed sword dance at a wedding.

His body was as fluid as any around him, his sword an extension of his arm, moving with him as he blocked and swung his weapon. . True, he did protect his injuries, but he still moved with a grace unusual in men. Enjoying the view, she was glad to be alone so no one could see her interest in the field of men

It was the next move that threatened to throw off her carefully planned movements, ones she'd designed carefully in case anyone watched her to see where her attentions lay.

Lewis held his hand up and stopped the parry long enough to remove his tunic. She nearly moaned with pleasure, but managed to control herself. Was he aware she watched as carefully as she did?

She didn't think so. Not once did he glance in her direction, his attention instead set on her father as he practiced.

How could he not be freezing in this weather? But he clearly was not since she could see the layer of sweat cover his rippling muscles as he engaged with her sire again. The man was built like a god, his dark red hair gathered by a leather tie that touched the top of his shoulders. A perfect length in her opinion.

So grateful she was alone, she allowed her imagination to take her to the forbidden place, picturing Lewis with no plaid wrapped around his torso, wishing she could see how he looked with nothing on at all. If she wasn't careful, she'd find herself with drool running down her chin.

"My lady. How do ye fare this morn?"

Jolted by the quick approach, she glanced up, surprised to see Duncan standing near her.

"I thought to keep ye company. Do ye mind?" He sat down before she agreed, but she decided to let it go. After all, he was a guard at Eddirdale Castle. What harm could he bring?

"Nay, I dinnae mind. I'm enjoying the weather out by the water." She waved her arm toward the coastline to let him now what drew her most.

"Och, 'tis a lovely view. But I notice ye are more drawn to the men in the lists. Ye are taken by Lewis?" His pursed lips told her he expected an honest answer.

The lad was a fool. "I watch my sire as he parries. I always carry a fear he'll take a wound to his side." The look she gave him dared him to argue her point.

"Of course ye would worry about him. I was about to go out and challenge Lewis, but I decided to visit with ye first."

As if he could parry with Lewis. He'd be flattened in a matter of moments. "Ye think ye are strong enough to parry with my sire or Lewis?"

He shrugged, a smug smirk crossing his face. "Of course I could, and I would prevail. Ye will see so soon enough."

"Go ahead. I'll gladly watch." She taunted him and he knew it, a sudden change in his expression there for a flash before he covered it. A look that said he'd prefer to choke her.

But he did something that took her totally by surprise. He grabbed her by the neck and yanked her toward him, his lips crushing hers with a revolting kiss that caused her position to change to one she didn't want, one that hurt. She squealed, attempting to push him away, but he held fast to her, trying to insert his tongue into her mouth.

She bit him.

And he made the mistake of daring to lift his hand as if he would slap her. She tried to duck, but unable to move far, she feared his hand would connect with the back of her head, so she brought her arm up to protect herself.

But she needn't have worried. Duncan took a fist to his face and went airborne, landing with a splash in the bay behind her. He flew so far in the air that she gasped, having no idea what had sent him so far in the air.

Lewis. "Are ye hale? Did he hurt ye?"

"Nay, he didnae hurt me. I'm fine, Lewis." She stuttered, unsure how to exactly handle the situation.

Her grandsire and father were directly behind Lewis.

"What happened?" her grandfather asked as a small crowd began to gather behind her.

Ysenda didn't know exactly what to say, not wishing to admit that Duncan had kissed her, that disgusting attempt to woo her so poor that she preferred to forget it.

Lewis' hands fisted at his side, but he turned to face her grandfather, squared his shoulders, and muttered, "He touched her."

Her grandfather shrugged and said, "Then he got what he deserved."

***

Lewis couldn't believe what Logan had said, but he wouldn't question the man. Frozen in the spot he stood in front of Ysenda, his heart beating so fast that he thought it would rip his chest open, he forced himself to calm down. She was hale and Duncan was gone.

He didn't understand what had come over him, but he'd heard her yelp in time for him to turn to witness Duncan forcing himself on her. Without another thought, he'd raced across the landscape to put his sword in his belly, deciding at the last minute that he'd rather feel the man's flesh against his so he dropped his weapon. He hadn't planned to toss him into the bay, but at least he wasn't a threat to Ysenda again.

Gavin pulled Duncan out of the water and dragged him behind him, stopping by Ysenda. "Apologize to my daughter."

"I did naught wrong," he declared, spitting out a mouthful of bay water. "She wanted my kiss."

Her father's face turned the color of a beet, and Ysenda looked uncomfortable as if she wished to take two steps back. Instead her father nodded to her grandfather and the two lifted him and hung him on a nearby branch, hanging by his tunic, his arms flailing.

Ysenda turned away, but not enough that Lewis didn't see her smile.

Her father said, "If ye dinnae apologize to her, I'm going to allow young Haggert here to use ye as an exercise in punching. I think he'd love some practice."

Unable to believe his ears, Lewis glanced over at Ysenda's father, who gave him a subtle nod. How he wished to get just one more punch in. The man was surely jesting, but then again, Lewis wasn't quite certain of anything. The Ramsays were different.

Her grandfather stepped forward and said, "How big a fool are ye, lad? He's already given ye a black eye that will tell all what happened. Want ye more? Mayhap he can knock out a few of those fine white teeth of yers."

Duncan spit out a mouthful of water then said, "My apologies, Ysenda." He spoke so fast she could barely understand him.

Her father stepped closer and said, "I couldnae hear ye."

Duncan glared at Lewis, then said, "Begging yer pardon, my lady. My apologies."

Ysenda only nodded, the pain now there on her

face, something else Lewis didn't like. After Gavin let Duncan down from the tree branch and set the fool free, he turned to Lewis and said, "Next time, warn me before ye turn away so quickly. Ye could lose an arm."

"There wasnae time, my lord."

"Ysenda, ye are hale?" her grandfather asked.

Ysenda nodded but Lewis knew it to be a lie. He barked, "Nay, I can see the pain in yer eyes. The bastard hurt her because he moved her. Ye cannae move her leg, fool." He took a step toward Duncan but Logan stepped in front of him.

"Ye've made yer point, Haggert. He'll no' come near her again."

Gavin dragged Duncan away, a small smile creeping across the elder man's face as he left.

Logan said, "I think ye should take her back to the keep, Haggert. Ye did a fine job protecting her. I'll get everyone out of here and ye take her back." Then he grinned and left.

"Lass, I hope he didnae hurt ye too badly." She'd looked so beautiful sitting here on her own, the firth behind her in its majestic glory, making her look as regal as any queen until the bastard had come along to ruin it.

Ysenda's eyes misted and she mumbled, "Please move my leg first, Lewis. He turned it oddly."

He scooped her up, freeing her leg from the odd position as he held both and asked, "Is this better?"

She nodded, wrapping her arms around his neck. "Please take me inside."

He headed back to the keep, his limping now barely noticeable, through the gates and across the courtyard, but her leg slipped so he hurried over to a bench near the edge of the courtyard, a place no one could see them. He set her down as gently as he could, settling her on his lap and propping her leg on the bench. "Forgive me, but I couldnae hold it up any longer. I'll return ye in just a moment."

She whispered, "No' yet."

Her lips met his, and he moaned as soon as he tasted her sweetness. Lost in all that was Ysenda, he angled his mouth over hers and kissed her back, his tongue tasting every bit of her. They'd kissed before but this one was different, a sense of urgency taking over him as if he feared she'd leave him.

She pressed her body against his, her breasts against his bare chest so hard that he could feel her erect nipples through the soft fabric of her tunic, her mantle having fallen away. Visions of Ysenda in the nude pressed against him nearly made him forget where he was, his hand coming up to fondle her breast inside the mantle. She responded with a squeal and arched against his hand.

But they were interrupted by a cough. He ended the kiss and the two turned to look at the intruder. Grif tipped his head toward the gates. "Gavin Ramsay headed this way."

"Many thanks," Lewis said. "Help me arrange her leg."

He stood up and Grif caught Ysenda's leg, and

the two arranged her so Lewis could carry her into the keep.

Ysenda, still in a daze from his kiss, or so he hoped, said to her approaching father, "We had to rearrange my leg."

Her father nodded and held the door for them.

Lewis peeked at Ysenda, who gave him a quick grin as soon as her father was behind them.

CHAPTER TEN

YSENDA'S MOTHER ARRIVED a few days later with Grandmama and her brother and sister in tow, shortly after the late meal. Fortunately, Errol was more than happy to join the Matheson men since he was only ten winters, and Eli, who was eight and ten, was happy to go anywhere other than Ramsay land. She had wished to go on patrol, but their mother had said no to having both her daughters on the same mission.

Eli came in first, followed by her mother and grandmother. Entering the room, Grandmama called out, "Are ye hale, Ysenda? Because if so, I'll see ye on the morrow. I have to go lie on a soft bed. Brigid, lead me to it. Ye know these old bones can ache something fierce after a long journey."

Her mother hurried over and gave her a careful but swift hug and then said, "I'll be back, Ysenda, once I find my chamber and settle my belongings."

Aunt Brigid fussed over her mother and grandmother, showing them to their chambers above stairs. Brigid and Marcas lived in the tower while Jennet and Ethan lived in a small cottage they'd built years ago. Tara's family took over the third floor, so there were plenty of chambers for visitors on the second floor.

Her sister marched over wide-eyed. When no one was listening, she leaned over and said, "What the hell is on yer leg?"

"Nice to see ye, Eli," she said.

Her sister's true name was Elisant, but the shortened name had caught on quickly. "Must ye always curse?"

"Hellfire, does it bother ye that much?'

"Aye."

"Fine then. What is on yer leg?"

Ysenda grinned while Eli rolled her eyes. "Some contraption Jennet and Ethan created to keep my leg from moving. Otherwise it could heal crooked."

Her mother flew back down the staircase and headed straight toward her, kissing her forehead and settling on a chair next to her. Her mother's thick, brown hair was free, full of waves from the plait she'd probably had it in.

Isla followed her down and said, "I'll find some food and set it on the sideboard. I'm sure ye are hungry."

"Any warm broth would be much appreciated, Isla. I'm frozen from that trip," her mother said. "The wind was fierce once we reached the end of the bay." She shivered and then grabbed a plaid from a basket next to the hearth, covering herself. "Ye dinnae need it, do ye, Ysenda?"

"Nay, Mama. I'm warm enough."

Her mother shivered. "With this cold, I may no' go back until spring! So tell me all. I need to hear it from ye. Da said ye were healing well, and Aunt Brenna told me to make sure her daughter has set ye up with something that keeps yer leg from moving. If ye move it too soon, then yer leg could heal crooked."

"I know, Mama. I'm being careful. I havenae tried to move on my own yet, but mostly because it hurts too much." She fussed with the small blanket she had covering her feet, which were elevated on a pillow-laden stool.

Her sister asked, "Are ye no' ready to run out the door yet? I'd be half daft by now."

Ysenda thought on her exact words. "Aye, I'm half daft. The other half wishes to keep the pain at bay."

Isla returned to the hall and handed out the goblets of broth. "Aunt Merewen, I filled it with veggies for ye. Ysenda doesnae like hers too full. And here's a platter of meat pies and fruit for ye all to share."

Even though Jennet and Brigid were not technically sisters, they'd been so close growing up that they acted like sisters. In fact, they all called each other auntie even if the term was not technically accurate. So, they were all aunts and uncles here on Matheson land.

The door opened and her sire entered, striding over to her mother and leaning down to kiss her cheek, using her pet name he often used. "The horses are all settled, Mere, and yer saddlebags are by the door. I'll take them up in a few minutes, but I'm quite sure I smell a meat pie. Their cook is wonderful. This smells like a beef pie too. I had lamb at the meal. I'll steal another and then run yer bags up."

Eli said, "Papa, ye are always eating. Dinnae eat all the fruit tarts. I want one too."

"I'll take a pie out to Errol, and then I'll return." He grabbed another and headed out the door, shouting over his shoulder. "I'll be back shortly, Mere."

Once it was just the four of them, Eli whispered, "I heard them saying that ye have a man interested in ye, Ysenda. They said Lewis was going to court ye, mayhap marry ye. Who is he?"

Ysenda snorted. "No' again. Lewis saved me. He dug me out of the snow in the avalanche, made a sled contraption to use to help me get out of the ravine and pulled me up with the help of Grif and Willum. 'Tis all. The two of us both went over the edge in the avalanche, and both had to be seen by the healers, but 'tis all there is to it. Naught more."

"If he's a nice man," her mother said between sips of broth. "Then mayhap ye should consider him. 'Tis time for ye to marry."

"Mayhap I dinnae wish to marry. I wish to go back on patrol. 'Tis why I've practiced for so many years." True that she'd always wished to go on patrol, but the recent truth of it had been less than appealing. She had to admit that staying here for a moon didn't bother her at all, especially during one of the coldest months of the year. But if she were hale and strong, she'd jump right back into her spot on patrol.

Hell, but why did everyone think a lass had to wish for marriage? Just because Reyna and Isla had married already did not mean everyone on patrol had to marry. How could they not see that she had been only interested in being assigned to an important group? The only problem was the persistent nightmares and fear of being caught on the ground in battle. She'd had a nasty one yestereve as soon as she'd fallen asleep, and it had left an impression on her.

Because of her nightmares, her battle preference was to be anywhere above the ground. But Dyna and Maitland both knew it, so she was always in a tree. Even her cousins knew it and accommodated her many times. In fact, Ceit had gone straight on once so Ysenda could climb into the branches. Everyone helped each other when they could.

"But ye'll no' be on patrol forever. Look at yer cousins. Isla is happily married and then going back on patrol, correct? And Reyna says the same."

Hellfire, but there was the truth. It was her cousins' fault.

"I'm no' interested." This was not a discussion she wished to have with her mother. Or should she tell her mother that another lad had introduced himself to her? How Duncan had flirted with her, though she had no interest in the lad. And he was too young. Like a wee bairn next to Lewis. It was probably better if she never mentioned Duncan to anyone or they'd have her married to him too.

Somehow, she guessed that her mother would hear all about Duncan and Lewis's wee disagreement the other day. It was something she wouldn't mention unless she was forced to for some reason. Of course, if she knew her sister, she would find out somehow.

But Lewis was far better looking than Duncan. And funnier. She supposed she'd compare everyone to Lewis now.

Her mother set her goblet down and crossed her arms, staring at her daughter. "Mayhap I missed something."

Ysenda asked, "What?"

She yawned, wondering what the hell her mother could be referring to. She'd hardly moved, so what could she be accused of?

"Ye look like hell. Have ye been sleeping?" Her mother's astute gaze traveled across her face, down her body, and back up again. "Ye've lost weight too. Are ye eating?"

"I'm trying to do both, but 'tis no' easy. The pain wakes me up every time I move at night."

Eli whispered, "How do ye pee?"

Her mother arched a brow at her in question.

She pointed to something covered with a piece of fabric, which was set in the corner of the hall behind a partition. "Aunt Jennet and Uncle Ethan made me a special chair with a hole in it. 'Tis right over there."

Eli made a face at her. "Everyone can hear ye there."

"I know. I have to wait until everyone leaves, and then Da carries me over there." She had to admit that she hated that part, but it was better than the alternative. She had one in her chamber too.

Eli gave a little squeal. "Da waits for ye? Right there?"

"Nay. He leaves and then returns when I yell for him. 'Tis most embarrassing."

Her mother finished sipping out of her goblet and set it down. "How long before ye can try walking again?"

Isla answered for her, and Ysenda did not mind one bit. If she uttered the words, she'd probably start crying.

"Mama said probably close to two moons."

"Two moons?" Eli's response came out as a shout. "Oh my heavens. Ye will be daft by then."

"I fear ye are correct." She refused to think on it, or she'd cry for sure.

Her mother drawled, "Ye may as well find that Lewis and have some fun with him. Ye'll be bored otherwise."

Isla looked at her and said, "Yer mother is right. Ye and Lewis get along, so why no' spend more time together? He's no' getting around easily either with two sprains, although ye would no' know it when he's around yer sire. 'Tis no' a commitment, but he could keep ye entertained. We canno'. Think on it. I was the same way with Grif. We argued more than anything, and now we're married and happy of it."

She hadn't looked at Isla's relationship that way, but now she realized Isla spoke the truth. "Ye did argue frequently. I remember. And I remember

Torrian warning Grif too. But ye argued. How can ye enjoy that?" Her relationship with Lewis was much different than Isla's relationship with Grif. They bantered more. Isla and Grif had hated one another. She liked Lewis, even enjoyed his company.

Isla clucked her tongue and laughed. "'Tis a fine line between love and hate. I know no' how else to explain it. And I think yer reaction to Lewis is telling enough that ye should spend more time with him. The two of ye get along. That much ye know already. Ye are way ahead of Grif's and my relationship. Ye've got naught else to do, so why no'?

Why not indeed? Perhaps she'd have to reconsider spending more time with Lewis. If she did, then mayhap she could get over thinking he was so handsome. Surely that would put an end to it.

Isla whispered, "There arenae many more handsome than Lewis, but ye know that already. Dinnae let him get away."

Get away? She hadn't considered that. It was time to rethink her time on Black Isle. But then she remembered Lewis' last words. He was not interested in her at all. And she was not interested in Lewis.

How long could she keep telling herself it was true?

CHAPTER ELEVEN

TWO DAYS LATER, Lewis stopped his horse in front of the cottage where he'd last seen his father and two sisters. He forced himself to focus on his task at hand, though he caught himself thinking on Ysenda too often, especially when it came to a lad named Duncan. He'd have to find a way to ask someone if she'd seemed interested in him. Grif. He'd have to find out what Isla said about Duncan.

Not now. He had to find his sire. Hellfire, when had he become the kind of man who only thought about women?

This cottage was where his family had lived, but he saw no signs of his sisters or his sire. A man was chopping wood out front. "What does a Matheson guard want with me?" the man called out to him, pausing with his axe still held in his hand.

The plaid Lewis wore and the sword he carried told everyone he was a Matheson guard.

"I'm looking for my sire. Goerge Haggert. He used to live here." Puzzled, he didn't have any idea where else to look for the man who called himself his father. He'd often checked on his sisters to make sure his sire treated them right, sometimes sneaking around at night so he'd not be seen, but he hadn't been able to once he went on patrol.

He chastised himself for not finding someone to watch over them. Where were they? Had the old man treated his dear sisters kindly?

But who could he have asked? He knew this had to change. Not knowing where Elspeth and Finella were started to churn in his belly. He had to find them. Mayhap he'd find a way to move them to Clan Matheson.

Without his father. Now that he was more familiar with the chief and his wife, perhaps he could ask for their permission for his sisters to be accepted into the clan. But first he'd have to find them.

The man explained, "He left early summer. Got in an argument with one of the neighbors down the row. Lazy arse, so they told me. I never met the man, just took over this place after he left. Took my wife and me a moon to clean it out after he departed."

Lewis couldn't argue with him about his father being lazy. He was. Made him do almost all the work except what his sisters could do. Elspeth would be twelve now and Finella ten. Lewis had that same old feeling of guilt overpower him for leaving his sisters with the old goat. But what could he have done for them? Their mother had died nearly five years ago, and the Haggert house had been unhappy ever since.

Not that his mother had ever been truly happy either. Their father was demanding and loved to yell. Fortunately for all of them, he left often, saying he was off to work, though none had ever been able to determine exactly what work he did.

Either way, he often returned with a sack full of food, ale, and some coin too. He never admitted where he gained any of it. Now Lewis had to wonder exactly where all those coins had come from. There could have been a reason they never knew what he did on his treks away from home.

"Do ye know where he went?"

"Nay, the neighbor went for the sheriff, so he left. Sent the girls to be nuns at an abbey, so I heard. Didnae want them any longer. The lasses are probably better off that way. That one was rotten to the core, I say."

The man returned to his chore, so Lewis turned his mount around and left, yelling back over his shoulder, "My thanks."

He had no idea where to go from here so he moved back to the main path that ran next to the bay and headed back to Matheson land. He rubbed his leg where the injury had been, still paining him some, but at least it hadn't been broken like poor Ysenda. She'd not find herself on a horse for a moon or more.

When he was halfway back, he stopped to take care of his needs, and planned to rest his leg for a few moments. It just was not completely healed yet. He probably should have stayed off a horse for another few days, but he'd felt compelled to go find his father.

Another horse approached and slowed, the rider dressed all in black. As soon as he drew closer, Lewis waved him down. It was Grif's brother. "Steinn, what brings ye here?"

Steinn stopped his horse and dismounted, making his way to Lewis' side. "Dinnae get up. Ye look like ye need the rest."

"I do." He continued to rub his injured leg. "I didnae know ye were here on Black Isle."

"I came back here after the patrol left. I figured Grif and Isla would return once the Yule came. I've just been riding about the Isle. 'Tis a mighty beautiful area."

"Aye, it is, especially along the coastline."

"Why are ye here?" Steinn sat down on a nearby boulder and then handed a skin of ale he had over to Lewis, who took a swig and returned it.

"I decided to visit my father and my two sisters, but he moved them all out of the cottage. The man living there now said he dropped the girls at an abbey. They could be nuns now, though I think they are a wee bit young for it."

"Do ye know which abbey?"

"Nay. I have no idea. And I have no idea where my sire would have gone." He heard hoofbeats approaching, and turned to see if it was someone he knew. "Grif?"

Grif stopped his horse, led him over to the other two horses and then joined Lewis and Steinn. "I heard my brother was around these parts so decided to come out looking for ye. Steinn, where the hell have ye been?"

"I traveled down the coastline. 'Tis so beautiful and I knew ye'd no' be here for a while with the storm in the south. Now I'm returning to Clan Matheson. Will yer wife allow me to join the clan?"

"Of course, Mathesons can always use new guards. Lewis, what are ye doing out here?"

"Ye two dinnae even look like brothers. Have ye ever been told that?" Lewis asked.

Grif's hair was brown, and he wore it long with a full beard. He was a large man with broad shoulders, not the kind of man you wished to run into in a dark night alone. Steinn, on the other hand, was thin, just a wee bit shorter than his brother, but his hair was blond, and he did not keep a beard.

"Even yer eye color is different. Yers are blue, Grif, while Steinn's are more green. Did ye have the same parents?" Lewis continued.

"Aye," Grif barked. "Mama's eyes were blue, and Da's were green."

Steinn added, "And sometimes, my eyes look blue too. They are a mix of blue and green."

Lewis sighed, making a quick decision. Perhaps it was time to tell all about what happened in his past. Grif could give him advice possibly. He dare not ask anyone else because he didn't wish them to know the truth. "I came looking for my sire. I wished to settle my past."

"And were ye successful?" Grif asked, picking up a pinecone and tearing it apart slowly.

"Nay. He moved and I have no idea where he is. The one who moved into our cottage said he took my two sisters to an abbey to be nuns. I dinnae know where they are either." He couldn't help but wonder if he'd ever see his dear sisters again. While they were quite a bit younger than his two and twenty winters, he'd helped raise them. He loved his sisters, and family was family.

Except for the cold-hearted father he had.

"Truly? Och, 'tis a shock for yer sisters. How old are they?"

"Twelve and ten."

Steinn offered, "If ye ask at a large abbey, then they usually know where the youngest nuns are. Ye could probably find them if ye set out to visit a few abbeys."

"And I may decide to do that, but I wished to speak with my sire." He paused, considering his words. "I worry for my sisters, but I also have a pressing matter to deal with. I fear the truth of my past will come out soon."

"What about yer past?" Grif asked. "Lewis, ye are an honorable, hard-working guard. I dinnae think there could be anything that bad in yer past."

"There is." He stood, pacing toward the firth. Hellfire, but he wished to find out the truth about what happened. Perhaps his friends could help him learn it, especially now that his sire was gone. He had to admit, there was no heartache over not seeing his father again. He'd been a mean old bastard most of the time. "When we lived at Clan Ross, I was accused of thievery. 'Tis why we had to move out. The chieftain said we had to leave, or he'd report my name to the sheriff."

He dropped his gaze, not wishing to see the derision in either of their gazes. Then, he picked up a handful of rocks, throwing them out over the firth, one at a time. Each one a little farther. As if he tried a little harder each time, things would work out.

"What the hell did ye steal?" Steinn asked.

He whirled back around to face his friends. "Naught. I didnae steal anything from anyone."

His fury caught him quickly but being falsely accused had never settled in his belly. He'd wished to argue, but his sire had said it was safer to move away. Said they couldn't risk the sheriff arriving and arresting him.

"What were ye accused of stealing?" Grif asked. "I know ye well enough to know ye didnae steal anything."

"My thanks to ye, Grif," he said after casting a side glance at Steinn.

"I dinnae know ye well enough to know that," Steinn countered. "So stop side-eyeing me. I went by what ye said."

He grinned at Steinn, knowing he was correct. It was Grif's opinion that mattered to him. "They said I stole a gemstone from the chieftain's brother's sword. The weapon was owned by their sire and had several rubies and sapphires in the hilt."

Grif whistled. "A ruby or a sapphire? Ye are lucky they didnae call the sheriff. I'm shocked they didnae," Grif said, brushing the dirt from his hands. "Did they have proof?"

"Nay, of course no'. I didnae do it, so how

could they prove it?" Lewis looked from Grif to Steinn. "I wished to talk to my sire to see what else he was told."

"What were ye told?" Steinn asked.

"I was only informed by my father. No one ever approached me about it, and we left the next morn. My sire wished to get me away before they changed their mind about the sheriff."

"And now I understand everything." Grif moved over to his horse, reaching for a piece of dried meat.

"What?" Steinn asked. "Because I dinnae."

Grif said, "It all makes sense now. Lewis is truly thinking about courting Ysenda, but he knows if her father or grandfather finds out that he was accused of thievery, they'd no' let ye near her. Am I right?"

Lewis couldn't deny that Grif had the right of it. "Aye, I am interested in Ysenda, though I know no' if she is interested in me." He couldn't admit that she'd said she had no interest in him at all. He liked to tell himself that her kisses and her response to his touch told him differently.

"Then, we'll go to Clan Ross and ask them. Mayhap they caught someone else after ye left," Steinn suggested. "We can go without ye."

"Nay!" Lewis jumped up from the boulder he sat on. "Promise me ye willnae. I'll find my sire first and ask him."

"Why no'? It would be easy enough to do. Ye'll get yer answer right away," Grif said.

"Because the chieftain said if he ever saw me again, he'd arrest me on the spot, then call the sheriff. I dinnae wish him to think I am in the area at all." His father had given him strict instructions to stay away.

Steinn glanced over at his brother, who gave him a subtle nod.

Steinn grumbled, but then said, "All right. We can help ye find yer sire, if ye'd like."

He paused for a moment, trying to decide how to exactly phrase his question.

"What is it?" Grif asked. "I see yer mind churning."

He decided it was best just to be straightforward. "Did Isla mention how Ysenda felt about Duncan?"

Grif grinned, but then Lewis said, "Enough. Just answer the question. I've got enough problems."

Grif let out a huge sigh. "Ye are correct. Isla said Duncan acted like a fool, and Ysenda would never be interested in him."

"Good. My thanks for yer honesty. Now back to my sire. I dinnae know how to find him."

Grif moved over and clasped his shoulder. "I'll be glad to help ye any way I can."

"I'll agree," Steinn said.

Lewis smiled. "I would like that, if ye dinnae mind. If I can prove I didnae do it, then I might ask Gavin Ramsay if I could court Ysenda."

Of course, he didn't tell Grif the biggest obstacle to his courting Gavin's daughter was the girl herself.

CHAPTER TWELVE

YSENDA JOLTED AWAKE and nearly
jumped out of her chair before the pain in
her leg stopped her and she yelped in surprise.

She managed to push herself up in her seat.
Apparently, she'd fallen asleep and they'd all left
her there. The fire in the hearth was down to
glowing embers, so she tugged the blanket up
over her shoulders and buried her face into the
soft fabric as she closed her eyes.

If she could only banish that nightmare from
her brain, then she'd be much happier.

She recalled having nightmares when she
was younger, but they went away. There was
no memory concerning what the nightmares
consisted of, but she knew they awakened her
at night screaming. Eli had slept in the same
chamber with her back then, and she'd always
woken Ysenda up with the same expression.
"Dammit to hell and back, wake up, Ysenda."

Ysenda had always awakened. The dream held
few memories for her, but the ones she'd had ever
since she'd gone on patrol had changed. Now
she had visions of a pair of animal jaws clamping

onto her arm. Sometimes, the jaws would clamp down on her leg, and even once, her head.

She had no idea what kind of animal it was. That was the oddest part of the nightmare. This animal, whatever it was, terrified her, yet chased her endlessly it seemed. Until it caught her, and the set of jaws snapped in front of her, ready to bite down. She never knew what happened after that because she always awakened.

Screaming. This is why she would never patrol on the ground. Horseback or tree was the only place she could feel safe. The only way she'd fight.

Lewis came down the staircase, a look of surprise on his face. "Ye are all right, lass?"

"Aye. Why do ye ask?" She rubbed the sleep from her eye, thinking she'd dreamed Lewis up with his hair askew about his head. But still as handsome as ever.

"Ye screamed, did ye no'?"

"Did I? I dinnae know. I just woke up from a nightmare."

He took a log from the nearby basket and threw it into the hearth. "'Tis freezing here. How can ye stand to stay here?"

She arched a brow at him because it was a ridiculous question.

"Och, aye. I recall. Ye canno' move on yer own, can ye?" Even in the dark, she could see the wry humor dancing in his eyes. How she loved that part of him. He loved to laugh and have fun, and his eyes always glittered with sheer joy.

She pursed her lips and shook her head.

"What was the nightmare about?" He stepped

closer and pushed a thick strand of hair off her face.

"I dinnae recall," she lied.

He chuckled. "Ye are lying again. Do ye no' remember that I can always tell when ye are lying?"

"Nay. Ye canno'." She glanced over at the hearth, watching the flames grow.

"And now ye willnae look at me. Another sign of lying. What was the dream about?" He sat in the chair across from her, leaned back, and folded his hands in his lap, looking quite satisfied with himself.

"It was about the man I'm supposed to marry," she said, crossing her arms.

"What did he look like?"

"Naught like ye."

"He probably looked like Duncan."

"Duncan? How did ye know?"

"Because he clearly admires ye."

"He didnae look like Duncan either. The man didnae look like either one of ye."

"I'm sure no'. I like to make sure I'll live a long life. I think if I were to sleep next to ye every night, I'd find a dagger in my side one day."

"Only if ye deserved it." She gave him a smug smile.

How she'd missed their banter. Before the avalanche, they'd spent all their time together bantering, teasing…anything but sweet words. It was just not in their nature. How she enjoyed their playful teasing, and she knew better than to take any of his teasing seriously.

So why had she believed him when he'd said he'd never consider marrying her? He had said it first, hadn't he? Or had she been the first to deny him? How she wished Eli had overheard the exchange. She would remember.

"Why would I deserve it? Do ye no' love yer husband?"

"I married ye because I had to, so I vow to wait until ye are deep in yer cups to roll ye off the bed and onto yer sword lying in just the right position at the edge of the bed." She made a sign of a sharp object coming across his throat to kill him.

Then, she closed her eyes and tipped her head to the side, her tongue hanging out.

"And ye are as lovely in death as ye are in life," he drawled.

"Whoever mentioned ye courting me has never been around the two of us, have they?"

"Nay, they would know that we suit each other as well as a big, old boar and a sweet, white horse."

"As well as a unicorn and a spider."

"As well as an adder and a princess."

"Or a wee puppy and a big stag."

"A priest and a nun."

She laughed at that one. "I'll be the priest. Ye be the nun." Now it was her turn. "A queen and prisoner who committed murder."

"A ripe pear and a chestnut."

"An angel and the devil."

This time he snorted. "I am no' the devil."

"Nor am I." She waited to see what his next response would be.

His gaze locked on hers, and he whispered, "We could be verra good together, but ye refuse to try."

"I doubt ye would agree. Something holds ye back more than what holds me back. I can see it in yer verra being." Shocked by how closely that statement was to the truth, she waited to see what his response would be.

He turned serious for a quick moment; she could see it in his jawline. He stood and then leaned over to pick her up. "I'll bring ye to yer chamber. I'm sure ye will sleep better there."

He was intentionally ignoring her last statement. She'd hit a sore spot. Something was holding him back, but he'd not admit it. She didn't know what to say to this serious side of Lewis. His eyes wore the look of pain, though she couldn't tell if it was emotional or physical.

Once he deposited her on the bed and arranged the covers, he said, "Ye are right. I have secrets, and if ye knew them, ye would never speak to me again."

He left her chamber, and she wished to call him back, though she knew she wouldn't. But somehow, she needed to learn his secrets.

One way or another, she'd find out.

CHAPTER THIRTEEN

L EWIS REGRETTED HIS decision to walk away from Ysenda last eve without answering her question, but he couldn't tell her the truth.

Would not tell her.

He was too embarrassed to let anyone know he'd been accused of thievery. If he'd been arrested by the sheriff, he could have had one of his hands cut off, a common consequence for young thieves.

He was falling in love with her, without a doubt, and he would not admit to something he never did. How he wished he knew the truth of the situation.

Striding out to the stables, he gave the stable lad instructions for his horse and then moved inside to see if Grif was there.

"Did ye think we would no' come?" Grif called out as he entered the stable. "Steinn is busy gathering any apples left on the trees in the orchard. If he finds enough, it will give us something to eat besides dried meat on our venture today."

"Isla didnae mind that ye'd be with us for the day?"

"Nay, she has enough family to keep her happy. She wished to spend the day with Charlotte, so it worked for us. The question is, which abbeys do we head to? Do ye know how many abbeys there are that house nuns?"

"Nay, but Ethan is always near the gates. I'll ask him. He may know more than we do." He pointed to Ethan a short distance away and called out to him. "Ethan, may I have a moment of yer time."

Ethan replied, "Ye may have two minutes. How can I be of help to ye?"

"My sisters were left at an abbey by my sire. The only problem is I dinnae know which abbey. Know ye of any abbeys with young nuns in the area?"

Ethan thought for a moment and then said, "Not on Black Isle. Mayhap Kirkhill. There is an abbey there, but I know no' if they house nuns. Ye may have to go to Inverness. There are several to check there. Find an inn to stay, and they'll tell ye where the nunneries are."

"My thanks, Ethan." He turned to take his leave, but Ethan stopped him.

"Ye have two sisters who wish to be nuns? 'Tis quite unusual."

"Nay, neither. My sire is a bastard. After our mother died, he had trouble managing the three of us, so I left. Apparently, he tired of my sisters and dropped them off."

"Cruel man."

"I'm surprised he took them to an abbey. I thought he cared for them, but apparently I was wrong. I checked on them for many moons, but once I went on patrol, I lost track of them." It was a sad thing to admit to someone, but Ethan was the type to accept his words for fact. He would not come up with any other reason for the truth.

"How old are they?"

"Twelve and ten."

"When ye find them, bring them here. We have many lasses here, as ye know, and we'll teach them to read. Isla loves to teach lasses."

"Many thanks to ye. I will consider it," Lewis said.

The stable lad approached with his horse, so he mounted and left through the gates, soon finding Grif on his horse talking with Steinn as they exchanged apples.

"What did ye learn?" Grif asked.

"We're headed to Inverness."

"Then we need to leave now if we have much searching to do. I wish to sleep in my own bed this eve. I told Isla I'd be gone no more than one night. My wife doesnae mind if I'm gone during the day because she's busy with her healing duties, but she doesnae like to sleep alone," Grif said.

Lewis chuckled. "Because ye put out so much heat by the size of ye. I'd wager she hates staying in that small cottage without ye."

Grif smiled at that. "Aye, she stays with Charlotte in her old chamber if I'm no' home. Says 'tis too cold."

"Hmph." Lewis had guessed that correctly. "I

hope we will be back this night, but it may no' happen."

The three set out down the main path that led off the peninsula, finding the roads mostly empty. Once they passed the end of the firth and rounded the edge to head toward Inverness, the path became busier. Come early afternoon, they made their way to an inn for a meal.

"Ye have the coin for some good food?" Steinn asked. "I thought I'd be eating apples all day." He grinned, a wee bit of excitement at the prospect of a fine supper overtaking him. "I know. My past is not full of cooked meals, so when it happens, I get excited."

"I dinnae blame ye," Lewis said, dismounting and tying his horse to a tree across the street from a busy inn.

The three made their way inside, surprised to see how large the dining area was. The owner pointed to a table for three and then sent a serving lass over to them.

"What would ye like?" she asked, a wide smile on her face. She stared first at Lewis, then Steinn, but eventually back to Lewis.

"What do ye recommend?" Lewis asked.

"The beef and barley stew is the best today." She gave Lewis a wide smile and tipped her head.

"Three trenchers of the stew, if ye please, and three ales." Lewis took his gaze from hers, somehow feeling as though any conversation with the lass would be disrespectful to Ysenda. Since she wasn't interested in any relationship with him, she could hardly be bothered by the situation, but Lewis was. Where had he gained his sense of right and wrong? Certainly not from his sire.

She nodded, moving toward the back of the building yet still staring at Lewis over her shoulder.

"She likes ye, Lewis." Grif clasped his shoulder and grinned.

"Nay, she was staring at Steinn."

Steinn snorted. "Aye, for five seconds. Then back to ye. Grif looks too old now."

Grif, clearly offended, said, "Never ye mind about me."

The owner strolled over, and Lewis caught him. "Can ye tell us where the abbeys are in town? And do any of them have nunneries?"

"Ye think ye can steal a bride away from a nunnery?" he drawled.

"Nay," Lewis barked back at him. "I'm searching for my sisters."

"Yer pardon. Ye are a Matheson guard?"

"Aye," Lewis replied. "We all are Matheson guards."

"And also on patrol for our king," Grif added. "Dinnae be rude."

The owner glared at him, then said, "There are only two nunneries. Go to the water's edge and follow it north. The abbey there has a nunnery, and the one at the far end of this road also houses nuns." He nodded and left them.

"Two places," Lewis said. "Should no' take us too long."

Once they filled their bellies, they left, heading to the abbey at the water's edge. They were stopped outside the tall gates.

A man came from the inside and stared at them. "What do ye want?"

"We're looking for two young girls. My two sisters were left at an abbey a short time ago."

"Not here. We do not have any young lasses. Only spinsters. Try the abbey at the far end of town." He walked away, ignoring them completely.

Steinn said, "I guess we head to the other abbey."

Lewis, discouraged already, said, "We have naught else to do but that. I hope they are there. If my sire went somewhere besides Inverness, we could be searching for days." And how he prayed it would not come to that. "The next closest place where they house nuns could be Edinburgh or Glasgow. Both are long trips."

Half the hour later, they arrived at the gates of the next abbey, one even larger than the abbey by the firth. Lewis stared up at the soaring central tower with a spire that looked to touch the clouds. Graceful cloisters surrounded the tower. Intricate stonework and detailed carvings in the surrounding wall were a testament to the hard work done by the old craftsmen.

"We've come to visit my two sisters," Lewis explained. "They were left here a short while ago."

The man was even more disagreeable than the last one. "They're no' here. Take yer leave. We dinnae like visitors."

He left so quickly they didn't have time to ask a question, but Lewis wasn't accepting of the man's rudeness. His boot caught the door before it closed and he entered, the man stunned to see him not far behind him at the door.

"Get out. Ye are not welcome here," the man said after he whirled around to face Lewis, his face reddening.

"Ye didnae answer my question. There are only two abbeys here in Inverness. I have already stopped at the other one and my sisters are no' there." Grif came up behind him so Lewis let the door fall on his friend while he strode toward the rude man. "Now, I will kindly ask ye again. And if I dinnae get the answer I'm looking for, the next time I ask ye, ye'll be hanging from the parapets."

The man backed up, but Steinn hurried in and ran to a spot behind the man. The man glanced over his shoulder at Steinn, just long enough to give Lewis the time he needed. He launched himself at the fool, shoved him against the cold stone wall, and placed his dagger at his neck.

"My sisters. One is named Elspeth and the other Finella. Have ye seen them?"

The man's eyes were so wide, he thought one was about to pop out of its socket. He nodded and pointed to the upstairs. "I'll get them for ye, my lord."

"Please do. Meet us in the back. I'm sure there is a courtyard under the trees."

"Aye, there is. I will bring them to ye."

Lewis' gaze searched the area, looking for any evidence of witnesses, but he didn't see anyone, so he took his leave after motioning to his friends to head back outside.

He had to admit his heart skipped a beat at the prospect that he was about to find his sisters. They made their way around the back, not surprised to see a young lad there to greet them. His poor sisters were left here alone.

What the hell was wrong with their sire that he would commit such an act?

"Bring yer horses and hide them over there." Then the lad disappeared.

Lewis had a wee bit of hope blossom inside himself, so he motioned to Grif and Steinn to take their horses. They were not bothered by anyone fortunately, so he moved to the back entrance.

The lad opened the door for them and said, "If ye sit in the courtyard for a few moments, I'll bring them to ye. The poor lasses are no' verra happy. My heart breaks for them."

"What is yer name, lad?"

"Adkin, my lord." Then, he disappeared inside the building next to the tall abbey.

He stared up at the spire while he waited. "I swear it touches the clouds, does it no'?"

Before long, the back door opened again, and two lassies ran out, both racing over to hug him. "Lewis, where have ye been?"

"We missed ye, Lewis."

Lewis stepped back and turned his sisters toward his friends. "Grif, Steinn, this is my sister, Elspeth, the taller one, and the other is Finella. I had no idea where ye were. Da just left ye here?" Then he motioned for them to sit on a nearby bench.

"Aye, he was angry. He tried to find ye, but then said he was going to leave us here to become nuns," Elspeth said, playing with her long hair in a plait.

Elspeth's hair had always had a dark red cast to it like her brother's while Finella's hair was more chestnut colored. Fi's was often curly, though hers was also in a tight plait.

Finella whispered, "I dinnae wish to be a nun. All they do is pray, Lewis. Can ye no' take us home? I'd prefer to play rather than pray."

He couldn't help but smile over his sister's request. He'd rather play too. "Och, I wish I could, but we have no home. I became a guard at Clan Matheson, but I've been on patrol for King Robert. And on Matheson land, I sleep with the guards. Though I hope someday to bring ye there so we can make it our new home."

Grif said, "If ye decide ye truly wish to leave, I'm sure ye would be accepted into Clan Matheson."

"Da is no' with ye? Then, where is he?" Elspeth asked.

"I have no' seen him. I was hoping ye could tell me where he is." Lewis thought the man would have told his daughters something concerning his whereabouts. Apparently, he dropped them here and ran.

Elspeth said, "I am glad ye havenae found him. I dinnae wish to live with him anymore. He became mean, striking us both for the littlest thing. He was upset, so he had to leave. He tried to give us to many people, but no one wanted us. It was terrible." Her eyes misted, and she swiped her tears away. "Even this is better than living with Da."

"When ye finish patrol, can we no' live with ye? I dinnae wish to live with Papa either," Finella said.

Lewis said, "I'll be on patrol for another few moons, then if ye like, I'll come and get ye. I'll bring ye with me to Clan Matheson. Ye'll like it there."

"Promise?" Elspeth asked, wiping tears from her cheeks.

"I promise. But I wish to find Da. I need to speak with him. Did he tell ye anything about where he was going?" How he wished he could take them now, but he had to settle the issue with his sire first. If he was ever to live a life unfettered with lies and doubts, he needed the truth now. He knew they were safe staying here, and Elspeth had admitted it was better here than living with their father.

A sad admittance indeed. He hadn't thought much on their predicament, but now he couldn't help but consider how it had been for them. He'd been able to leave, but they'd been forced to stay on with the mean bastard. And the fact that they admitted he'd started hitting them stung his pride. He should have gone back to check on them more closely. He vowed to make their lives improve once he settled issues with the mean old goat.

The fact that the brute had tried to pass them off to a neighbor was even more painful. Yet no one had wanted them.

He knew what it felt like to be unwanted. Ysenda had basically declared that much to everyone in the great hall, and that had stung his pride too. But to have your sire send you away?

Both girls shook their heads. "He said he had to get away because he was in trouble."

"Aye, I heard that he argued with a neighbor, so he left."

"No' exactly." Elspeth glanced at her sister, who nodded.

"What? Please tell me the truth, Elspeth," Lewis said, taking her hands in his.

"Papa stole from the man. He accused him of stealing some food from his garden and something else he had hidden in the back of his house."

"But Da denied it, did he no'?" He had a feeling that there was so much more to the truth of his father's behaviors. Had he been stealing for years? Is that how he'd gotten their food?

She nodded sheepishly and glanced over her shoulder as if the man stood behind them. "Aye, but I saw him sneaking in the man's backyard. It was after the man left to go to market. He snuck over there in the dark of night and came back with a big smile. I had to pretend that I didnae see him, but I did. I think he stole the man's coin. The man said he was calling the sheriff, so we left the next day."

Lewis thought his head was going to explode. He hoped he'd taken something from the neighbor because he didn't wish to see his bairns go hungry. Many years ago, his father had said he was borrowing something from a friend and that he would repay him. Could that be the situation here? He couldn't blame someone if there was no other possible solution. Perhaps he'd spoken with the neighbor and had been given permission to take what he needed. Or he'd like to hope that his father had no food left in the house and the girls were hungry. Was that why he'd gone into the neighbor's yard? To feed his children?

He had so many questions for the man.

He had to find him, now more than ever. He wanted the truth. It was entirely possible that he'd learned who the guilty party was many years ago. If so, Lewis deserved the truth.

He just had to find the man first.

When they left, Lewis said, "Grif, I hope ye dinnae mind, but I'd like to search a few places for my sire along the way. He could be hiding in any dilapidated old hut. He'd not join a clan. Of that much, I'm sure. He cursed out Clan Ross forever. So if ye dinnae mind, I can start the search on the way back and get ye home to Isla on the morrow. I have to believe that he isnae far away from here. I think he likes to keep an eye on the lasses and me. He probably heard that I joined the Matheson guard."

"Do ye truly think he'd looking for ye?" Grif asked. "For what purpose?"

"I have a new theory. Da is desperate. He does no work, so how does he eat? I believe he couldnae feed my sisters so he left them in search of some scheme for a lazy arse to steal coin. I think he's done so his entire life. But he no longer has me as a scapegoat."

"Unless ye find him. Then he could do it again. Are ye sure ye wish to antagonize the man?" Steinn asked. "He doesnae sound like he has any moral constitution."

"'Tis true. Every word ye say is true, but I must hear it from his lips."

"That he lied to ye? That someone else stole the gemstone?" Grif asked.

"That *he* stole the gemstone and gave the Ross chieftain my name. He lied about his own son." While he'd never had strong feelings for his father, a new one blossomed in his heart.

He hated the man more than ever.

CHAPTER FOURTEEN

YSENDA HADN'T SEEN Lewis in a few days, but time marched on. The next group of travelers arrived, and she couldn't have been more surprised. Her parents were both here along with her grandparents, but a few days before Yule they were all surprised by Torrian and his wife Heather along with Nellie and Lucas.

But the biggest surprise was when Aunt Brenna came through the door.

"Aunt Brenna!" She wished to run to her, but she wasn't quite up to that yet.

Her beloved aunt came right to her side after she greeted her own daughter and granddaughters, Charlotte, Isla, and Jennet.

"I must get warm somehow, lass, so I'm sitting next to ye in front of that hearth." Her smile was as warm as the heat in the flames, making Ysenda feel special just because her aunt was here.

Jennet hurried out of the hall and called over her shoulder, "I'm getting ye some warm broth, Mama. I'll be right back."

"And a fruit tart, if ye please," Auntie called out. "I'm famished."

Ysenda did her best to sit up but struggled. It was so much easier when Lewis was here to move her up or her sire, but her father was always out in the lists, training the Matheson guards.

And then there was Lewis. She had no idea where he was. Isla had only said to her, "He's gone to Inverness with Grif. They'll probably return later. Grif said they wouldnae be long."

That was the day before.

She reminded herself that Lewis had made it clear that they would not be courting. And she'd agreed, though she hid the lie well. Lewis had a life of his own that didn't focus on Clan Ramsay, so she did her best not to be offended by his comments.

Aunt Brenna leaned her head down to put her cheek to Ysenda's forehead.

"Fear no', I must always check for the fever. Ye feel fine. It has been nearly a moon by now, has it no'?"

"In a few days, aye. It doesnae hurt as much unless I knock it," she explained. "How long will I have to be in this contraption?" She couldn't stop the tears from misting her eyes.

It had seemed like an eternity that she'd been stuck in this chair by the hearth. The hearth, her chamber, the hearth, her chamber. Her sire had carried her outside twice, but that was it.

"Now listen, lassie. I know it seems like forever, but ye cannae risk making that bone crooked. It will follow ye through yer entire life. But here is why I came along. We brought a cart loaded with different items, and one of them is a contraption that Uncle Quade, God rest his soul, created for someone else who had a broken bone. I think it was Gregor many years ago, but it will allow ye to walk a wee bit on yer own without putting any pressure on that bone. Ye must be at least three sennights out from the break, and ye are there, so I think ye can try it. 'Tis like a walking boot. The armorer helped him make it. Yer gait will be verra uneven, but ye can walk slowly. I'll help ye with it on the morrow once we empty the cart. I have gifts for everyone as well. Where's Gwyneth? I expected to find her near the hearth too."

"Grandmama is around somewhere."

"I'm here," Ysenda's grandmother answered. "I'm bringing the fruit tarts because I knew ye would be wanting one. And this poor lass has hardly moved, so I'll help ye get that device in here on the morrow."

Charlotte came over and hugged Aunt Brenna again. "Grandmama, are ye staying for Yule?"

"Of course, I'll be here for Yule. All of us will be."

Brigid came down from above stairs and said, "We'll have the most wonderful Yule this year. We'll hang the greens on the morrow, and the men will go hunting. I hope for a nice, plump pheasant this year, Mama."

"Dinnae look at me for that. Merewen and Ysenda...or no' Ysenda. Merewen and Isla can hunt for pheasant and mayhap a nice, big goose.

Though ye all know Logan wishes for a big, fat boar to roast out back."

"Mayhap we'll have them all," her aunt Brigid said. "We'll cook lots of pastries too. I'll make a fine stew with a wee bit of each meat. Marcas loves it when I mix them together. Mutton, beef, pork, even duck and rabbit."

Ysenda had to admit that seeing everyone together like this was wonderful. And the thought of being able to walk, if even for a wee bit, was most exciting. If she had her way, she'd push for it to happen this evening, but even she could see how tired her great aunt was.

And Aunt Brenna had always seemed tireless.

Heather came in with Nellie, and before she knew it, there was a circle of chairs around the hearth. Everyone jested and laughed about everything and anything—the trip, the bairns, and the food. Everything.

Jennet gave her a goblet of ale, so she drank it down quickly and then rested her head back, listening to all the voices as they lulled her to sleep. She hadn't slept well last night, so she was not concerned if she snuck a wee nap in front of everyone.

Her eyes were closed, but she heard pieces of the conversation.

Aunt Brenna to her mother: "How has she been? Jennet, she has not walked on it at all, has she? Ye know how important it is."

Brigid said, "Aunt Brenna, we didnae allow her out of the chair for any reason."

Her mother explained, "Gavin carried her into her bed every night."

Charlotte giggled and said: "After she pished in the chair over there."

"Charlotte." Her mother chastised her cousin appropriately.

She sighed, thinking tomorrow would be a better day. The voices all melted into one.

Then the door burst open, and the wild beast came in, headed straight for her, its jaw opened wide and its sharp teeth dripping saliva. It was coming for her.

She screamed and screamed, swinging her fist at the monster, but he wouldn't let her go.

"Ysenda, lass. 'Tis me. Please dinnae punch me again."

She opened her eyes, surprised to see Lewis standing there with Grif behind him giving advice. "Wake her up. She's having a nightmare." The hall was dark and empty. Where had everyone gone? She leaned her head back and closed her eyes again, too tired to lift her head.

"Ysenda. Wake up."

Her eyes flew open and scanned the area, but there was no beast. "Where is it?"

"Where is what?" Lewis asked, his hands holding hers. He knelt in front of her, so he was eye level with her.

"The beast."

Grif called to him from the staircase, "I'm finding my bed. I canno' keep my eyes open. Wake Gavin if ye wish. He'll take her to her chamber." Then he changed his direction and headed to the kitchen instead. "I'm hungry. Then I'll go out the back way."

Lewis' voice was as calm as she'd ever heard it. "There's no beast here. And if there were, I would never allow it near ye." He brushed the loose hair away from her face. "Ye are cold out here. The fire is barely embers. Shall I take ye to yer chamber?"

"Aye, please. I dinnae wish to be near that door." She had an image of the monstrous animal charging through the front door, making its way to her.

He scooped her up, lifting her like she weighed no more than a hummingbird.

"Where is everyone?" she asked.

"In bed, if I were to guess. Ye had visitors, I heard, but 'tis the middle of the night. We just returned from Inverness. Traveling by the light of the moon is slower than daytime."

He opened the door to her temporary bedchamber and set her down on the bed carefully, helping to prop her foot up so it would not hurt her. "How's that?"

"'Tis fine. Many thanks to ye, Lewis."

To her surprise, he leaned down and kissed her forehead. She pulled him back, kissing him on the lips instead. "Please dinnae go. I'm afraid."

"No one will bother ye, Ysenda. The guards are at the gate. No one can come inside the hall, or they'd see him."

"Or it." She took a sudden chill and began to shake, something she couldn't stop.

"Ye are trembling. Are ye that cold?" he asked, rubbing his hands down her forearms.

"Aye. I'm frozen."

"I'll put one log on, but 'tis all. I'll no' have a fire here in the middle of the night."

"Then hold me until the chamber warms. Please? Ye have so much more heat than I do, Lewis. Please?"

He sighed, played with the fire, and then came back to the bed. "For a few moments only. Ye know what would happen if anyone caught me here in yer bed?"

"Who would catch ye? Everyone is asleep. Once I stop trembling, ye can take yer leave."

"All right." He scooted in next to her and she snuggled against him, sighing when his warmth spread through her. "Ye are like a chunk of ice on the loch, lass."

"I know. I need ye." She snuggled against him.

"Just for a few moments," he said. "Tell me who came this eve."

Ysenda started to recite all the names but then recalled her good news. "Aunt Brenna has a new contraption for me, so I can walk a wee bit. I'll get it on the morrow." Her eyes fluttered shut, but then she opened them quickly, pleased to see Lewis was still here.

His eyes fluttered closed, but she knew he was still awake, so she snuggled against him again, closing her eyes.

They both fell sound asleep.

CHAPTER FIFTEEN

L EWIS AWAKENED, SURPRISED to see a wee bit of light in the chamber. Ysenda was firmly ensconced against his chest, but the bad part was that the sun was coming up.

And he was still in her bedchamber. His head jerked up as a realization came to him.

He was not just in her bedchamber but in her bed.

He was in Ysenda's bed, under the covers and with his arms wrapped around her.

Hellfire.

He did his best to climb out of bed without moving her, but he failed. She stirred and whispered, "Dinnae go."

"Lass, 'tis morn, and I must go before yer sire catches me here, or worse, yer grandsire."

"They willnae care. Ye kept me warm."

"I fear they'll know that. I'm leaving. Take care. I'll check on ye later." He gave her a quick kiss on her lips then crept over to the door, opened it, and stepped outside.

Directly into the path of Logan Ramsay.

"Gwynie, I'll either be stringing him up by

his bollocks or finding a priest. Which is it to be, Haggert?"

"Logan, leave him be until ye find all the facts." Gwyneth Ramsay sat by the hearth, sipping on a cup of broth.

Lewis spit words out so fast he couldn't hear himself. "Naught happened. I swear to ye it was innocent. I had to help her to bed—she was alone when I came in." Hell, but the sweat was dripping down every part of his body even though the hall was freezing because the hearth hadn't heated the place yet. "She was cold out here. The fire was barely embers."

Gavin came out of the kitchens and stopped in his tracks as soon as his gaze fell on Lewis. "Ye are coming from my daughter's chamber?"

"Naught happened. I helped her into her bed because ye all left her out here."

Gavin caught him by surprise, launching himself at Lewis, grabbing him by the neck, and throwing him against the wall. "I'll kill ye for touching her."

Logan bellowed, "Gavin, I'll handle it. Hold him while I get the rope to tie around his bollocks. I'll string him up in the courtyard for all to see."

"Da! Grandda! Help me!" They all heard Ysenda's shout and all three raced into the chamber, but Lewis was there first.

"What's wrong?"

"Naught with ye. Da, leave Lewis alone. He helped me into my bed. 'Tis all it was. Why did ye leave me there alone?"

Logan came around the bed and put his face in front of hers. "Lass, do ye forget that I was just outside the door when he exited yer chamber? How long were the two of ye here together? 'Tis either string him up by his bollocks or find a priest."

Ysenda picked up a pillow and swung it at her grandfather. "The hell ye will. Ye'll no' be forcing me to marry anyone. Who do ye think ye are?" Her voice continued to rise as she hit her grandfather, though he backed up enough to be out of range.

"What the hell did I do? Gavin, control yer daughter." Logan Ramsay whirled around and bellowed, "Gwynie, ye need to calm this lass down."

Gwyneth entered the chamber and said, "Gavin and Logan, get yer arses out of here now."

Gavin looked at him and said, "I'll kill ye later, Haggert. Ye are no' escaping this. On yer honor, ye will marry her. Ye've compromised her, and I'll not let it go."

Gavin and Logan both left, and Lewis stared at Gwyneth Ramsay and then at Ysenda. "I'm sorry, Ysenda. I just wanted to warm ye until the fire started…"

"I know that. Grandmama, he did naught wrong. Ye all left me out there to freeze, so he brought me in here to go to sleep only we both fell asleep. He was riding all night from Inverness. Leave him be."

Brenna came into the room, Ysenda's mother behind her. "What is happening?" Merewen asked. "The look on Gavin's face was not a happy one."

Ysenda pushed herself up a wee bit. "Da and Grandda are being daft, 'tis all there is. I'm no' marrying Lewis whether they wish it or no'."

Logan stuck his head around the corner and explained, "I came out of the kitchens to see Haggert leaving her chamber at dawn. What would ye have me do? I know what the hell Quade would do, and ye'll no' change my mind, either one of ye. Her reputation's been compromised."

"Only if ye think it so, Logan. And only if ye tell everyone. Ye are the only ones who saw it." Brenna fisted her hands on her hips and said, "Get out. Now."

Merewen moved next to her daughter, away from the two arguing. She motioned for her husband to leave.

Logan took a step back, a look of shock on his face, and said, "Did ye just try to tell me what to do, Brenna Grant?"

She stepped closer to him and said, "I did. I ordered ye and Gavin to get out. Do it, or I'll grab yer bollocks and twist them. I dare ye to test me."

Logan didn't move, the two elders of the Ramsay clan glaring at each other, but Gavin turned and ran out the door.

"Logan, ye get one more warning." Brenna took another step closer to Logan, but he cursed under his breath, turned, and then left.

"We'll discuss this in the hall." The old warrior was still grumbling once he stepped out.

Ysenda said, "My thanks, Aunt Brenna. Nothing happened. I had another nightmare, and I woke up screaming. Lewis had just come inside. I was cold because the fire had died. He brought me in here, and it was freezing in here too. I was shivering. He just warmed me, and we both fell asleep. I swear, Mama, nothing else happened. Please dinnae embarrass me."

Merewen patted her hand and said, "We'll get ye over by the hearth, get some porridge in yer belly. Then we'll get that new contraption for ye so we can get ye moving today."

Brenna looked at Lewis and said, "Ye look a wee bit stronger than Merewen or me. Will ye please carry her out to her chair by the hearth? I'll guide the leg."

"Aye." He couldn't hide the sweat dripping down his temples or down the middle of his back. In fact, he was quite sure that his tunic was drenched with sweat by now.

And if they could see his arse, they'd see naught but sweat there too. He'd never been in such a heated position as the one that had just transpired. All he wished to do was disappear. He'd carry Ysenda out and then beg to take his leave.

In fact, when he walked out through the door, he didn't even dare look at her because she had a death grip on his arm as if he'd drop her. He whispered, "I'll no' drop ye, lass."

She didn't let go, but then again, once he stepped into the hall, he understood why. Every one of her family had to be in the hall.

And they all stared at the two of them.

He strode by Torrian Ramsay and his wife but slowed to say, "Greetings, Chief." Then by Marcas and again he stopped, "Morn to ye, Chief, and to yer wife."

He'd met Torrian when they'd started patrol, so he had to show his respect. Then, of course, he said the same to his own chieftain.

Marcas and Brigid, Jennet and Ethan, Tara and Shaw, Gwyneth and Logan, Gavin and Merewen…Isla. They were all here along with various wee ones.

Torrian said, "Heather and Nellie, would ye mind taking the wee ones above stairs for a bit. Take the tray of fruit and a loaf of bread with ye."

"Absolutely." Heather hurried over to Ysenda's side and kissed her cheek, then left the hall with the bairns behind her while Nellie grabbed the platter of food.

And Lewis knew there was only one thing he could do.

He set Ysenda down with Brenna's help, strode over to Gavin, and then waited until everyone quieted.

"My lord, if ye feel that I have compromised yer daughter in any way, then I accept it and will do the honorable thing and offer for her. Ye have my word that she has no' been compromised, that was never my intent, but I understand how the situation looks. I am fond of Ysenda and will marry her if this is what ye wish."

"I appreciate that, Lewis. I think there will be a wedding soon." Gavin crossed his arms and looked to Merewen.

Tara interrupted, "Nay, ye are no' doing this again. Ye all just tried to make my brother marry Ceit before they were ready, and ye nearly drove them apart. Marcas, ye'll no' force this.

As far as Lewis was concerned, hell came over the entire group because within a few moments, everyone was yelling.

Marcas announced, "I didnae force anything."

And the comments flew so fast, he didn't even know who said what. His head darted from one person to another, trying to take it all in.

"'Tis Logan's fault."

"I'm the one who caught them. At least someone knows the truth." Logan crossed his arms, his gaze locked on Lewis.

"Mind yer own business, old man," Brenna declared.

"Stop trying to ruin everyone's life," Gwyneth shouted.

"Leave them be," Tara said.

"I will once they are married," Logan replied.

"Get the priest." That was the only comment Gavin made, and Lewis had to admit he didn't like it one bit.

"The hell ye will," Brenna said.

"Stop ordering people around, Gavin," Gwyneth said.

"Ye dinnae control everyone," Shaw said.

And the arguing continued.

He glanced over at Ysenda, who looked as uncomfortable as anyone, but he could see the tears about to burst out. He nearly moved to her side, but Brenna looked straight at him and gave him a subtle shake of her head.

If he trusted anyone, then it was Brenna.

"Nay, ye willnae!"Ysenda then let out a scream that reached to the rafters, and everyone turned to face her. "Good. Now that I have yer attention, I'll tell ye what happened. I fell asleep before ye all went to bed, apparently, then ye all left me here to freeze in the middle of the hall by myself. And I had nightmares again. Those blasted nightmares that I hate. Lewis was just returning from Inverness and was heading above stairs when he heard me screaming. So, he woke me up, kept me from falling out of the chair because I was so frightened, and then put a log in the hearth. Once I calmed down, he took me into my chamber." Then, she paused to stare at all those around her. "Something ye all forgot to do. It was so damn cold out here that I thought I'd have frostbite. And my chamber was even colder. So, he carried me to my bed and then put wood in the fire, but as ye know, it takes a while to heat up. Ye do realize that I am totally helpless?" She waited for anyone to answer, but no one said anything.

Ysenda grabbed a nearby plaid and covered herself. "I shivered so badly that he wrapped his arms around me to warm me.

"To. Warm. Me. Nothing else. And we both fell asleep. The next thing I know, my grandfather is threatening the poor man for helping me."

Brenna asked, "What is yer nightmare, Ysenda?"

She held her arms up to silence everyone else. "I'd like to hear it from her."

Ysenda sighed, but she continued. "I've had the dream for a long time, but it is becoming more persistent. And more clear. I used to dream of monsters chasing me, but I could never see them. Last eve, I dreamed of a huge beast with long teeth, its jaw trying to bite me in the face. It nearly did, and I began to scream to get it off me. Lewis was here."

"None of what ye said excuses that he came out of yer bedchamber this morn," Logan said.

Gavin said, "I agree with Da. We need a priest. Ysenda, ye're getting married."

Merewen started to argue with Gavin, and then Gwyneth yelled at Logan. The entire group began to argue again, Ysenda began to cry, and then Brenna set two fingers between her lips and let out a shrill whistle.

"Ye all better listen to me and listen well." She looked at Gavin and Logan and Torrian and everyone else, one by one. "Now, I'm going to put myself in that poor girl's position."

She moved over to another chair, grabbed something to lock her leg above the chair, not moving. "Merewen, wrap my leg with those plaids, please."

Merewen did as she instructed, then stepped back.

Brenna barely managed to keep herself still, but then she pointed to Logan. "Now, ye two wise arses. Which one of ye would like to come over here and demonstrate how a man could compromise a woman in this position."

Gavin and Logan both stared at each other wide-eyed.

Logan said, "Brenna, ye are being unreasonable."

"Nay, ye are. That granddaughter of yers would have so much pain from any movement that it could never happen. Come over here now. Try and show me how it could be done."

"Brenna, ye know if there is a wish for it, they'll find a way," Logan grumbled.

"Mayhap until a lass screams in pain. And that lass would be screaming. Her private area is nearly covered in metal, for heaven's sake."

Logan covered his ears at the word 'private.' "Saints above, Brenna. Use some discretion."

"Logan Ramsay, ye've tested me many times over the years, but I swear this is yer worst."

The old warrior just glared at her.

Tara began to giggle. "Nicely done, Aunt Brenna."

"Gavin, ye wish to show me how the man compromised yer daughter?"

"Ye made yer point, Auntie."

Brenna hopped down off the chair. "Good. Now I'd like to help yer daughter get out of that contraption and into the one I brought. Will ye help me?"

"Aye," Gavin and Merewen spoke at the same time.

Logan turned to leave. Brenna called out, "Logan, no priest. Do ye hear me?"

He mumbled but kept going.

"Logan Ramsay.Ye heard me, but I dinnae hear ye."

"Nae wedding."

"Gavin?"

"Agreed."

Marcas looked at Lewis and said, "Ye may take yer leave."

Lewis let out the breath he'd been holding and then glanced over at Ysenda, who tipped her head toward the door.

Marcas clasped his shoulder first and said, "Nicely done doing the honorable thing. That will no' be forgotten by anyone. Take yer leave while ye can."

"I understand, but with my history, I dinnae think the Ramsays would welcome me into the clan. I'm no' worthy of Ysenda."

"Can ye elaborate on that thought, Lewis? I know naught of yer history that would make that statement true."

Lewis fumbled for words but then said, "I have naught to say at this time, Chief. Mayhap when I return, I'll have more to tell ye."

"Understood."

"I have one question for ye, Chief, if ye dinnae mind." He pushed himself because he could not stop thinking about his dear sisters sitting in an abbey feeling unwanted.

"Go ahead," he replied.

"When I finish with patrol, would I be allowed to bring my two sisters to Clan Matheson? One is twelve and the other is ten."

"Where are they now?"

"My sire left them at an abbey with the nuns."

"And yer sire and mother?"

"My mother passed away years ago. My father has disappeared with no promise to return."

"They are welcome whenever ye wish. They can sleep in Charlotte's chamber. She would love it."

"Many thanks to ye."

He headed out the door only to run into Grif just outside.

"I'm heading off to search for my father. Would ye be willing to travel with me again? And the laird says I can bring my sisters back with me, so I'll be bringing the lassies along when I return."

"I'd be happy to go with ye. I'll see if Steinn will join us." He scratched his beard, a pensive look crossing his face.

"What's wrong, Grif?" he asked his friend, not liking the look on his face.

"We just received word that Maitland needs help. His two nephews have been kidnapped."

"Nephews? How old are they?"

"Five and three."

Lewis let out a low whistle. "Are ye leaving? We can search for my sire after we find Maitland's nephews. Lads that age need to be found right away. My sire has been a bastard for years. My trip can wait until we've settled Maitland's issue."

"I have to talk with Isla. I'm going to help him however I can." Grif explained. "And then I'll assist ye in whatever way I can."

"I'd be pleased to help ye with Maitland's problem. There is no more need for me to stay here. I assume they are on Menzie land." Lewis was more than happy to leave Matheson land after all that had transpired.

"Aye. 'Tis the Menzie chieftain's lads."

Lewis said, "I'll go, but we may not arrive in time, so I truly do hope we are too late, and we'll find them safely at home. I had planned to head out in search of my sire, but this is more important."

Steinn came up behind Grif. "I'll go with ye, Lewis. Grif, go see what Isla says, but I'm ready to go."

Lewis said, "I'll be ready also. Everything happens at once, it seems. But we can manage the two issues. And I'm more than happy to take my leave from Matheson land for a wee bit." He rolled his eyes for effect. He'd be pleased not to set eyes on Logan for a while.

Grif grinned and clasped his shoulder. "I'm hearing tales already in the stable. The yelling was quite loud and heated. We'll chat later."

Lewis headed to the stable, hoping to hide from the two Ramsays. He had no idea where they were or if they would jump out and attack him again.

It was sheer instinct that made his hand go down to guard his bollocks.

CHAPTER SIXTEEN

———— ❧ ————

High sun, outside Eddirdale Castle by the bay

ONE MAN SAID, "She knows. Ye must tell her."

"I'm not telling her anything." The older man said and then spit off to the side.

"Ye better. She's having nightmares because of it. She'll remember eventually."

"She doesnae recall it, and I'm not telling her. I suggest ye keep yer mouth shut. Naught good will come of it."

The younger man paced in a circle then stopped in front of the other man. "Ye have one day to tell her the truth. If ye dinnae, then I will. Ye dinnae scare me, old man. This is about more than loyalty and honor."

The older man narrowed his gaze and said, "Ye are a fool. Some secrets should stay that way."

CHAPTER SEVENTEEN

YSENDA DIDN'T KNOW whether to feel bad or good about the entire situation.

Tara came over and helped her to sit up. "Come. Aunt Brenna has taken the men out to unload the cart. I'm sure she has things to help ye. I canno' wait to see her contraption. It will be wonderful to feel a wee bit more natural than the device ye've been in."

She didn't know whether to cry or rejoice about what had happened. In fact, she could feel the tears misting her gaze.

Tara patted her forearm. "The same thing happened to Ceit. They tried to force her to marry Brin because they stayed in the cave together. It was life or death. Ye canno' be cold in this weather, or it could kill ye. Ye canno' move, so that makes it even more dangerous for ye, but they are too bull-headed to understand that simple truth. But as ye know, Ceit and Brin married a short time ago, and they are verra happy. 'Tis important not to force things on young people. My mother said her mother made Alex promise not to force marriages on his sisters. So Aunt Brenna believes the same. 'Tis only right that if men can choose their spouse, then women can too. Ignore yer grandfather. He's a stubborn old man who loves ye and wants what is best for ye, just as yer sire does, but his old ways of thinking often get in the way."

That didn't stop her need for a few tears.

Aunt Brenna entered with her father behind her. "Gavin, just set it next to her. I'll arrange it and see if I can get her to walk."

"I'll stay and help," her sire said.

Ysenda did not want him here.

Aunt Brenna took one look at her and said, "I think I know what the problem is."

Tara frowned but said nothing.

Ysenda stared at her father, wishing him away.

"Gavin, since I have to undress yer daughter to change the contraption, I think ye should go. And dinnae let anyone in the door for half the hour."

Her sire looked immediately uncomfortable and then said, "I'm leaving."

"Here? Ye will undress me here?" Ysenda must have heard her aunt incorrectly.

Tara said, "I'll get the partition. It will hide ye completely, and I'm sure yer sire will no' let anyone enter. But the partition will make ye feel better. Then, if we can get this to work, can we not get her in the tub this eve, Aunt Brenna? We could have it put in her chamber in front of the hearth."

"Aye. We'll get her used to this and then a bath this eve. First, I have to remove yer leggings, lass, so I can check the bone."

Tara added, "Oh, and Aunt Gwyneth gave me a new pair of leggings for ye. She made them extra soft and stretchy. Extra room to maneuver yerself. Here," she took a package from a pile she'd brought in and set on a nearby table. "See if ye like this pair."

Ysenda took the leggings out and ran her fingers across the fabric. It was a rich brown color, like the color of her favorite horse, and soft with lots of stretch in it. "I must thank Grandmama. These are more than fine."

Aunt Brenna helped her remove her leggings, leaving her tunic on while Tara arranged the partition perfectly. "I think I know what the problem is, and now that yer sire is gone, I'll ask ye."

"Go ahead. Ask me whatever ye wish," she said honestly.

"Ye do like Lewis, and he likes ye, but ye are worried the situation with yer sire and grandsire may have driven Lewis away. Do I make sense?" Aunt Brenna asked.

"Aye," she admitted with a deep sigh. "He'll probably hate me now, and we are just friends. He's always teased me on patrol, but now he'll probably never talk to me again."

Tara said, "Ysenda, I think yer feelings are returned. The man offered for ye. I dinnae think he would do that if he didnae truly like ye. Dinnae worry on it."

Aunt Brenna said, "Though dinnae expect him to return quickly. I suspect that Logan scared him enough that ye'll no' see him for a few days. Even though a man has feelings for ye, he will no' like to be forced into marriage any more than ye do. Men act oddly when it has to do with their bollocks."

"But where will he go?"

Tara shrugged her shoulders. "Who knows? Wait and see for sure."

"But for now, I'd like to check yer bone," Aunt Brenna said. "I'll start off soft, and ye tell me if it hurts ye." She took her two fingers and ran them down the front of her shin and over to the back of her leg where her bone had been broken.

"Tara, where was the break exactly?"

"In the bone in the back. About one-third of the way down from the knee."

Aunt Brenna pushed carefully on her skin, following the bone down in her lower leg. "Does it hurt at all?"

"Just a wee bit in one spot." Ysenda couldn't believe how much better her leg was, giving her hope that she could be free of this restrictive position soon.

"Tell me when." She repeated the same movement and waited for her to tell her when it was sore.

"There. That spot is a little sore, and I think 'tis exactly where the worst pain was before. I'm surprised it has healed that much."

"Tara, did ye do this or Jennet?"

Jennet came in the door and called out over the partition. "We both did, Mama. I did my best to set it straight, and Tara checked me. How is it?"

"Beautiful. Ye did a fine job, ladies." She ran her

hand down the front of Ysenda's leg. "'Tis smooth as can be. Feel it yerself. 'Tis no' hurting her."

Ysenda couldn't help but get excited. "Then I can walk on it now?"

Three voices said in unison, "Nay!"

She frowned, uncertain why they reacted so strongly. "But ye said it was healed."

Aunt Brenna explained, "Nay, 'tis healing, not healed. This is a big step and it has a great start. I'm always pleased when it starts to heal straight so I dinnae have to break it again and straighten it." Her aunt's hand continued to travel down her leg, checking everything over.

"Ye would do that?" The thought of such a thing made her wish to heave.

"To make sure yer leg is straight for the rest of yer life, aye. But they did a fine job, so we can move along to the walking contraption."

"It looks like a big boot," Tara said.

"It is. I had the armorer make it. The thing ye must remember is that yer leg will no' be able to move inside it. We canno' risk breaking the bone again, so ye canno' move it about. It must stay still, and we dinnae want ye to put all yer weight on it yet. I'll give ye a walking stick to bear some of yer weight. And I also need ye to know that ye have not been walking on the other leg at all, so it will surprise ye when ye try to walk on it. In fact, it will try to tell ye no' to walk on it because it has had no muscle movement to speak of. So, yer muscles will try to say no walking. But ye must start to move the good leg slowly. 'Tis a gradual process."

Jennet added, "And never, never dismount from a horse for at least another moon."

"Another moon? How will I go on patrol?"

"Yule is coming, so there will be no patrol for at least a fortnight. 'Twill not be an issue for ye yet." Jennet added warm water to the basin. "Mama, remember when one of the guards didn't believe us about being careful?"

"Ye mean the time he jumped off his horse and snapped the bone worse than the first time?"

"Aye. 'Twas a sad day for both of us. His because of the pain, mine because it was harder to fix." Brenna shook her head with a smile. "People are fools sometimes."

"I willnae be a fool. I promise, Aunt Brenna. I'll do whatever ye say," Ysenda said. She would do anything to get herself out of the contraptions and this restricted life she'd been forced into.

Tara said, "Mama and I saw something similar on Cameron land. A guard who didnae wish to listen. So he started walking on both legs, then he fell down a knoll and broke it again. Not worse, but the same break. He had to start all over again. He cursed out my mother until Papa came in and punched him. Papa rarely loses his temper unless it's over Mama."

Aunt Brenna washed her leg with the fresh water in the basin Jennet had brought with her. Once she dried Ysenda's leg, she said, "All right. I'm going to put this on yer leg, and then we will all help ye to stand."

Ysenda wished to cry with excitement, but

instead, she giggled. "I'm excited. Forgive me, Aunt Brenna."

The three arranged the contraption and tightened it. "How does that feel? It should be tight, but it should not be painful," Aunt Brenna explained.

"It doesnae hurt," she replied.

"Tara, ye stand on that side of her. Jennet on the other side, and I'll stand in front in case she topples. When ye stand, Ysenda, put most of yer weight on the good leg."

Ysenda nodded, then leaned forward and let Tara and Jennet help her.

She fell almost immediately, but they caught her.

"What happened?" her aunt asked.

"My good leg buckled. Why?" Panicking because she thought it wouldn't work, Ysenda resolved to beg her aunt to try again if she had to.

"Because ye havenae used it in a moon. Yer good leg will adjust; ye just must take it slow. Try again but give Jennet more of yer weight."

She tried again and managed to stand up, her weight on her good leg and leaning against Jennet, who held her for now. "'Tis a verra different feeling."

"All right, walk a few steps with support until ye are accustomed to the movement, then Jennet will step away, and we'll give ye the stick on that side."

She did as they suggested, and even though she stumbled a few times, she finally got used to the odd contraption and managed to walk with the cane and without putting any weight on her broken leg.

She smiled, hope blossoming through her. Her bone was healing, and she was going to take a bath this eve.

The only other thing she wished to do was find Lewis.

She had to apologize for all that had happened.

CHAPTER EIGHTEEN

LEWIS, GRIF, AND Steinn left later that day. He couldn't get away from Logan and Gavin fast enough. It showed in his pace.

"Slow down, Haggert, or yer horse will never make it." Grif caught up with him but nodded toward his panting mount.

"I know. I'm far enough away now." He had a difficult time explaining how the Ramsay elders had affected him. Or was it just that he didn't wish to admit it? Either way, he kept it to himself.

Steinn chuckled. "They're no' coming for yer bollocks. I promise. And if they do, we'll protect ye."

His hand almost moved to protect his private area, but he controlled the urge. "I know. We can slow down." He patted his horse, hoping to calm the beast a wee bit.

Grif pulled his horse abreast of him and asked, "Would ye have been that upset if they'd have forced ye to marry her? Ye like her; we all know it. Everyone but ye two."

"Aye. I dinnae wish to be forced. I'm no' saying

I may not wish to marry Ysenda someday, but I dinnae think she would have been happy anyway."

They'd just traveled around the end of the firth and headed down the main path. "I hope the snow is gone on the ravine," Grif said.

"It should be. There have been no storms since then." Steinn stared up at the clouds overhead. "It should be clear all day."

They made it across with no trouble, but they were surprised to see Dobbin headed their way. "What now, Dobbin?" Grif asked. Dobbin carried messages back and forth between the clans and also helped with the patrol.

"They found the lads. Killed the bastard who was trying to get the bairn."

"What?"

Dobbin told them the story of Maitland's brother but ended it with the best story. "Och, I nearly forgot. Maitland married Maeve Grant."

"Truly?" Lewis asked, stunned. He looked to Grif, who was nodding with a smile on his face.

"I dinnae know Maeve, but I'm happy for Maitland. He deserves some happiness in his life."

"But will he still run the patrol?" Lewis asked, hoping he would continue. He felt verra safe with Dyna and Maitland.

"He says aye. Maeve may stay on Menzie land depending on where the patrol is going. He says ye'll hear from him once the holiday is over. Now I must hurry home. Da always brings the orphans from Ayr to our home for Yule. He always finds a few. I'll leave ye at the fork in the path."

They chattered on until Dobbin took his leave for Castle Curanta. No sooner had he left when Steinn asked, "Now that we are three again, I have a question for ye, Lewis. Did ye compromise the lass?"

Grif bellowed, "Steinn. What the hell is wrong with ye? I know ye are a few years younger but dinnae be stupid."

"'Tis a fair question. I need to learn." Steinn lifted his chin a notch, then looked to Lewis for an answer.

Lewis said, "Nay, I dinnae."

"But ye thought about it," Grif said with a smirk on his face.

"Aye, I did for a brief moment, but Brenna was correct. She said with that contraption she had on her leg, there was no way. The lass has been in serious pain ever since the avalanche. Every single time she moved she was reminded of it. I feel awful for her. I tried to kiss her once in the healing chamber, and I fell off the stool. Then we were both in pain. It didnae work."

Grif chuckled. "Wish I'd been there to see when Brenna went after Logan. I heard it was priceless. That neither Gavin nor Logan could argue with the woman."

"'Tis true. And she was right. If no' for that, she could have been compromised. But she was also as warm as the ice on the loch in January. That was also discouraging."

"Ha," Steinn snorted. "That would no' stop me."

Grif and Lewis both looked at him and laughed.

Grif mumbled, "Ye'll see someday. 'Tis far easier in the summer."

"So," Grif said once they stopped laughing. "We'll help ye find yer sire, but where would ye like to look? Now that we are no' headed to Menzie land, where would ye like to go first?"

Lewis stopped his horse, thinking on his father. How far would he run? Would he go away from his daughters or closer? Would he leave the Highlands to get away?

"How much coin do ye think he has? Would he go to Edinburgh or Glasgow?" Grif asked.

"Nay. My sire was a gambler too. He thought I didnae know, but I heard one of the neighbors talking about it. There was a place not far from Clan Ross where he would go and gamble. Lost quite a bit, or so I was told. So where could he gamble?"

"Inverness. There would be more gambling in any city," Steinn said. "And I doubt he would go all the way to Edinburgh just to gamble. There are too many opportunities in Inverness."

"I have to agree with ye," Lewis said. "My sire would want to be able to hide well, and he would borrow from as many people as possible."

Grif pointed toward Inverness. "Then 'tis where we head. Because if 'tis true, then he will wish to gamble and borrow often."

Steinn added, "There are many fools who will loan ye money in Inverness. And if ye dinnae pay it back, ye may find yerself on a ship on yer way to Europe. I've noticed wherever ye see a fleet of ships, ye'll find men willing to gamble their coin away for various reasons. And they have the advantage of getting one in their cups and throwing them on the ship if ye cross them."

Grif added, "Or tossed off a dock somewhere. I agree with Steinn. We check Inverness first. And if we dinnae find him, we ask the gamblers in Inverness where the next closest spot would be."

"I dinnae know exactly where to start in Inverness, but there are plenty of gambling houses along the way," Lewis said. "I'll find the bastard."

"Anyone who gambles knows the other gamblers in the city. Someone new is easily recognizable. Ye'll find him if he's in Inverness."

"Grif, do me a favor."

"Anything, Lewis."

"Stop me from killing him, will ye? The more I think on his act of leaving my sisters in a nunnery, the angrier I get. How could the man treat his own flesh and blood like that? And I fear once I start punching him, I may no' stop." He'd thought on the situation more and more. He could forgive the man for stealing food to feed two wee lasses, but leaving them at a nunnery, never to return? What a cruel act for two lasses so young. There was no excuse for that behavior.

"Ye have my word."

Lewis sighed. In his heart, he knew one thing. If he ever wished to court Ysenda, then he needed to clear his name and that meant finding his sire.

He would not stop until he found the evil bastard.

CHAPTER NINETEEN

YSENDA PRACTICED AND practiced until she felt confident enough that she wouldn't fall. Aunt Brenna checked on her often to make sure she was not causing herself any more problems, but she was pleased with her progress.

But Ysenda had two issues that would not leave her. First was her nightmare. It didn't stop, instead continuing to bother her more and more. Each night, she awakened bathed in sweat, visions of a beast with huge teeth attacking her. She had no other clues as to why she had the nightmare.

She wished it to leave her forever.

The second issue concerned Lewis. Where was he? Why hadn't he returned?

She knew he had left with Grif and Steinn, and since all three were Matheson guards, she thought Marcas might have an idea, so she made her way out to the gatehouse three days after Lewis had disappeared.

Fortunately, Marcas came down the stairs from the curtain wall and headed straight toward her.

"Uncle Marcas, may I have a word?"

"Of course, Ysenda. Ye are doing well with that new device. How does it feel?"

It hurt, but she would hide what she could. The device freed her from so many restrictions that she wished to continue using it. "'Tis an odd feeling, but at least I can make my way outside and around the hall on my own. I didnae like being dependent on others." She didn't wish to be limited to a chair in the great hall again. After finally being able to move on her own, she wished to continue to improve, not work backwards. And everyone had fussed over her enough. She would not let on that she still had wee bits of pain for fear one of the healers would suggest she wasn't ready yet. The bone pain was so much better than it had been in the beginning that she had to believe it was improving.

"That makes perfect sense. Why do we no' make our way over to the bench under the tree over there. 'Tis out of the way of most ears."

"May I lean on ye?" Sometimes it was easier to use someone's shoulder rather than the stick, especially if that someone was a strong man.

"Absolutely."

He helped her to sit, and she breathed a sigh of relief. Walking was a great pleasure, but it also tired her. "I'm wondering if ye know where Lewis and Grif are? They left a few days ago, and I thought they would return by now."

"Interested in Lewis, are ye?" He arched a brow and waited for her response.

"I need to apologize for the issue the other day. I asked him to keep me warm that night. 'Twas my fault." She blushed but didn't give any more explanation.

"How much do ye know about Lewis?"

"No' much. Only that he was at Clan Ross before he came to Clan Matheson, but that was long ago." Her curiosity had piqued over the question.

Was Lewis hiding something?

"I'm going to be honest with ye. Even Lewis doesn't know that I am aware of his family's wee problem. I have no' told him."

"Problem?"

"When he was at Clan Ross, he and his family were sent away. Ross did no' tell me why, but if I wished to pursue it, I could probably learn more. I hope that if I ask Lewis, he'll tell me all. He's been an honorable guard so I have no' taken it any farther. But if ye wish for an easy way to convince yer sire and grandsire that ye wouldnae make a good couple, we could use this as a reason."

Stunned by this information, she wasn't quite sure how to respond to it. Except she didn't believe that Lewis could have caused their expulsion from a clan. "I believe Lewis is an honorable man. Ye have no idea why they were sent away?"

Uncle Marcas held his hand up for her to pause. "Nay, I am unaware of the reason. Howbeit, it has come to my attention that his sire was living in a cottage in a small village not far from here, but he left that area because a neighbor accused him of stealing his coins. He left without arguing about it, so I assume the accusation to be true."

Ysenda couldn't believe what she was hearing. "His own father was accused of thievery? Could the same have happened at Clan Ross?"

"It is possible, but I will not jump to conclusions over this matter. I believe Lewis still seeks the location of his sire. I know not why, but he did ask me if he could move his sisters here."

"He has sisters? Where are they?"

"I believe he said they are ten and twelve and that his sire had left the two of them at an abbey, with no promise of returning. Lewis wishes to bring them here. Charlotte would be pleased to have two more friends so I would welcome them."

"Oh my. I wouldnae be happy if I discovered my sire had done the same." Poor Lewis. She couldn't imagine what he was going through. "Does he know which abbey they are in? Is that where they have gone?"

"He did leave with the intention of helping Maitland find his nephews, but they were found a while ago. He is out there looking for his father, and I expect when he returns he'll have his sisters with him. The journey could take a while."

Ysenda stared across the courtyard, in shock over what Lewis had been going through. No one in her family or clan would ever do something like that to her. A man deserting his children? It was unthinkable. She wondered what Lewis would do when he found his father. How did one fight against their own sire?

"Do ye need anything else, Ysenda? May I escort ye inside?"

"Nay. I think I'll try practicing my archery. I have no' used a bow in a long time."

"Just be careful."

"I will," she said, pushing herself to a standing position. "Uncle Marcas, do ye know when he will return? Did ye tell him they needed to be back any time special?"

Uncle Marcas shook his head. "I canno' tell ye that, but I can tell ye one thing for certain."

"What?"

"If either yer father or yer grandfather hear anything about Lewis and Clan Ross, I am quite certain yer grandfather will head straight to the Ross chieftain to find out the truth. And that could guarantee they'd never force the marriage. If ye need a reason to make them stop pushing it other than Aunt Brenna, ye have one. Use it wisely. I'll not betray him yet."

She wouldn't either. Not yet. But she'd save it just in case she needed it later.

<hr>

Lewis had spent two days in Inverness searching for his father to no avail. There was one more large inn near the water that they hadn't tried yet. He prayed they'd learn something about him.

They had already heard multiple stories about one man who was new to Inverness. He'd borrowed and gambled plenty already, but he had an uncanny way of disappearing when his payment was due.

He'd also been accused of stealing by two people already.

His name? Lewis Haggert. That was the name he gave.

Grif said, "I have to start calling ye something else, or ye could verra well get arrested."

"Nay, he willnae. The men who were robbed know it was no' Lewis who robbed him," Steinn declared. Then he glanced at their friend. "But mayhap ye should come up with a new name."

"Just change yer name while ye are here," Grif said. "What would ye like it to be?"

"Mayhap ye are correct. If I'm known on Ross land and in Inverness, I probably should change my name," Lewis said.

He scratched his beard, not used to having it this long except when he was on the road or on patrol. Even then he had to trim it every few days with his dagger. It bugged him otherwise.

"Who did ye admire? Any uncles or relatives ye admired?" Grif asked.

"Like Uncle Ellar?" Lewis asked sarcastically.

They all knew the man had turned on Grif, getting him arrested for something he didn't do. The old man had his reasons, but Grif did not agree with him.

"Ye take that name, and I'll punch ye first," Grif drawled. "Though I'd know ye were sick in the head if ye did."

"I had an uncle I liked once. He died when he was young. 'Samuel.'"

"Sammy it is," Grif declared.

"No' Sammy. I said 'Samuel.'"

Steinn chortled, but they continued. "The last chance. This is the inn. Shall we go inside?"

Lewis looked at the inn, one that was much larger than any of the others. Since it was not far from the port, the inn probably took in many travelers or so Lewis assumed. Or would it be the men from the ships? The oarsmen? The Norse? Who would they see most often?

Grif stepped inside first, followed by Steinn and Lewis. "Dinner," Steinn said. "I'm starving. Have ye the coin for a nice meal?"

"I have enough," Lewis said. "I'll pay."

He'd saved his coin over the years from what he'd earned as a guard. Not much, but he had little to spend it on. Matheson's gave him all he needed. Also the reason they didn't make many coin.

They sat down, and a serving lass came over and asked, "What can I get for ye?"

"Yer finest stew for three," Lewis said. "And a fresh loaf of bread. What is yer flavor for the day?"

"Lamb or beef?"

"Beef, if ye please."

"Anything else?"

"Three ales," Grif added before lowering his voice. "And my friend Samuel here will pay. Ye have any gambling on the premises? We have the coin."

She nodded before she left. "In the cellars."

Lewis said a quick prayer that he would find his father. He needed to hear the truth from the man's lips. That he had given his sisters up without any plan of returning for them. He deserted the two lasses. One couldn't sink much lower than that. And that he'd been accused of stealing by a neighbor. And then he deserved to hear the truth about Clan Ross. How Lewis wished to learn the truth about that situation. Would he ever know?

They ate their meal silently, mostly because Lewis had too much on his mind. Once he asked, "What if he's not here?"

Grif said, "Simple. We go back to Matheson land and regroup. It's nearly Yule. Who knows where he is? If he's no' here, then he's no' in Inverness."

"I need to get my sisters first. I promised them."

"Without any protection along the road? Two young lasses?" Grif glanced over at his brother, who'd stared at Lewis wide-eyed.

Steinn added, "I dinnae wish to be the only one to protect them. There are many reivers about near Yule. Ye know of it."

"We've no' had any trouble yet. We can protect two lasses. We'll dress them like lads." Lewis didn't want to think of his dear sisters alone in an abbey for Yule. It was the time to be festive, even if it never was in their home. It was time for Finella and Elspeth to learn how everyone else lived.

"And if we see trouble brewing?" Steinn asked.

"If we see trouble before we get them, then we'll go back to Matheson land and see if Marcas will send a few men with me."

Steinn snorted. "Logan Ramsay would probably help ye, Samuel. Or Gavin."

"Hell nay!"

He wanted to be as far away from that old man as he could. Taking a swig of his ale, he scanned the dining hall, still hoping to see his sire, but there was no one there he knew. So, he took his last bite of his stew and then finished his bread. When he raised his gaze again, he nearly shouted, but he kept control.

His father was headed straight toward him.

"Da?"

The man pulled a chair out and sat down. His hair looked as if he hadn't washed it in days, and he had dark circles under his eyes. His gait was unsteady, depending on the furniture to hold him up. His back had become hunched over in the short time Lewis had been gone. How long had it been since he'd seen the man? Clearly, his life had been difficult if his present condition was any indication.

"Pleased to see ye again, Lewis."

He almost told his father he didn't use that name, but he caught Grif's eye as the other man gave him a subtle shake of his head. True. If his sire knew he was using "Samuel," then he'd just accuse Samuel of being a thief. Better to keep that part private.

"Da, what are ye doing here?" Would he admit to being in the cellar gambling? That had to be where he came from. He didn't expect his father had the coin to stay in an inn as nice as this one unless he'd gained a large pile of winnings.

"I came to Inverness to look for work. I was told the wharf was the best place to look so here I am. All these ships here. There's bound to be some work somewhere."

"And have ye found work?" He couldn't help

but stare at his father, to watch him as the lies slipped from his tongue so easily. How had Lewis never guessed before?

"Aye. I've done a wee bit here and a bit there. I've got some coin. What brings ye to Inverness?"

"Work for Clan Matheson. Where are my sisters?" He had to see if his father would lie to him or tell the truth.

His father cleared his throat, something he did often when he had to create some lie. Why was it a surprise that the man was a thief when he'd worked so diligently at lying? So much of his life before he'd joined Clan Matheson was beginning to make sense to him. Why they traveled on occasion, but always had to hurry home and take the roads less traveled. How he often said he'd visit someone again, but they never did.

He probably stole something from every person they ever visited.

Or how things would materialize at home and Lewis would wonder where they came from— ten tallows, a bag of vegetables that hadn't been there the day before. Or the watch his father had begun to wear one day. Lewis had asked him where it came from, and his sire had told him he'd always had it. He'd just decided to use it for a few days.

Would he tell the truth about his own daughters?

"I left them at one of the abbeys. Elspeth wishes to be a nun, so I left her there, and Finella didn't wish to leave her, so she stayed too. I'll go back and check on them at the end of winter once I have enough money to find a place to live again."

Lewis didn't believe a word the man said. Lies. All lies. They came from his lips as if he believed them to be true.

His sire leaned forward and said, "I need to apologize to ye, Lewis. I made a big mistake a while ago, and I need to make it right. I lied about something."

"Truly? And what is that?" he asked, wondering what lie his father was going to spew now? He decided to let him go and allow him to keep lying before stopping him. Let the old man hang himself with his words.

"I told a lie to the chieftain of Clan Ross. I told them ye were the one who stole the gemstone."

Stunned that his father would tell the truth, Lewis stared at him, waiting for him to continue. Was he finally feeling some unknown need to be honest? After all this time he was willing to admit he'd stolen the gemstone instead of Lewis?

His father looked him in the eye and said, "Yer sister stole it when she was playing with the laird's daughter one day, and I didn't wish to have her arrested. She was too young. And she is still stealing, so the abbey is the best place for her."

The man was beyond reprehensible. Lewis didn't even wish to tell him that he knew the truth because it wouldn't matter to his louse of a sire. "And what happened at the other cottage ye were in?"

"I wanted to come to Inverness. I caught yer sister stealing again, so I decided it was time to make a change. Thought I could make more coin here. I had to do something to try to put a stop to her stealing. I'm hoping the nuns will teach her right from wrong. Even if they have to take a switch to her, she should learn that stealing is against the law, even in God's eyes. Look, 'tis rather late, and I'd like to speak to ye about another business venture I've been offered. Where are ye staying?"

"Here. We're getting a room here," Lewis answered.

Grif got out of his chair as soon as Lewis made the statement and moved over to speak to the innkeeper, most likely arranging for two rooms, if Lewis were to guess.

"Would ye mind paying for an extra chamber for me? We need to talk. Then, I'll be on my way on the morrow, and ye can go on as ye planned. I'll no' be any bother. My room is on the other end of town."

Lewis knew that to be a lie. If he were to bet, he'd wager that his father was sneaking into the stables and sleeping there at night. He looked a mess. But the man was still his father, and Lewis would get the truth from him.

Even if he had to beat it out of him.

"Sure, Da. I'll get ye a room. But only if we get the chance to speak privately."

"I promise," the man said with a smile.

He didn't want to kill him in front of witnesses.

CHAPTER TWENTY

LEWIS AWAKENED IN the middle of the night, stewing on the conversation he'd had with his sire. Da had been very convincing when he discussed Elspeth's choice to become a nun and if Lewis himself hadn't spoken with the lass just days ago he may have believed his father's lies. But the blather about Elspeth stealing the gems was simply nonsense. Lewis had known that his father was a lying fool, but tonight's conversation still stunned him.

He got up and headed to his father's chamber, knocking lightly and not surprised to see the door open quickly. "Ye are awake?"

"Aye. Thinking about ye." His father wouldn't look him in the eye, a sure sign that did not bode well for his thoughts.

"What about me?" He didn't expect an honest answer, but he wished to hear what he would conjure up.

"Come in. Ye can have the chair."

There was a small chest with a basin and one chair in the room. His father sat on the bed.

"Da, I know ye lied. I know it was ye who

stole lately and that's why ye were driven from yer cottage. So I must ask ye. Are ye the one who stole the gemstone and who gave the chieftain my name instead at Clan Ross?"

His father stood so fast that he hadn't seen it coming, his arm swinging in a wide arc and slapping his face hard. "Ye ungrateful cur. I told ye it was yer sister who stole. I dinnae like where yer mind is going. Mayhap 'tis time to do something for me. After all I've done for ye, ye owe me."

He rubbed the spot where his father slapped him, and he struggled to contain his emotions to keep from grabbing him by the neck and choking him. He knew he didn't owe the man anything, but he was a convincing liar. Lewis decided to hear the man out first before he told him he knew the truth. This would allow the old fool the chance to spin another web of lies.

"What do ye want from me?" He wouldn't do anything to help the man, but he was curious as to what he had in mind.

In fact, he was regretting his decision to pay for the man's room. He should have walked away from his sire. He'd never confess the truth.

His father began to wring his hands before he paced the room. "I met up with a group, and we have plans to raid the wealthy on the path from Inverness to Edinburgh. They've done it for many moons now and have found it to be quite successful, but they need more protection. I've agreed to help, but I told them I'd find my son, who was a fine swordsman, and he would protect us."

"Protect ye? When ye're stealing?" Lewis gaped. The man's audacity never ceased to amaze Lewis.

His father swung his arm out to hit him again, but this time, Lewis was faster. He grabbed his father's hand and stood up, crushing his hand into a fist. "Nay, no' again. I've lost all respect for ye."

His sire jerked his hand back and flexed his hand in and out of a fist. "Ye hurt me."

"Good. Now get on with it. I need some sleep."

"Fine. Ye will ride to protect us, and I'll give ye ten percent of what I make."

He reminded himself that now was the time to get all the information he needed on his sire's group. "How many men would I have to protect?"

"Could be a score. One or two dinnae always go with us, but this is a large heist, so I expect them all to be there."

"And how can I protect a score of men on my own?"

"Ye need to fight off the guards that the nobleman will have around him. Ye are more skilled than any of the men I'm with so I need yer assistance in seeing this happen. And yer two friends also."

He laughed at that. "I'm not a thief like ye, so the answer is nay." He got up and reached for the door handle. It was time to be done with the man. End the relationship. He would retrieve his sisters and never look for him again. The time to end the relationship was now. He knew that Grif and Steinn would never help his father.

"No' so fast. Ye might want to hear the alternative. And dinnae think to tell me about yer friends and how honest they are. I've seen the one wandering about town as much as any reiver. He'll gladly assist me."

He spun around, not trusting his sire for anything, waiting to hear what his offer would be. His insult was probably directed at Steinn because he had been wandering for a while.

"Ye have a choice. Ye go with me, or I'll have to sell yer sisters to the men."

"I know where Elspeth and Finella are. I'll get them myself so I know this is a lie also."

"Do ye? Then did ye see the men I hired go back to the abbey to retrieve them? I have them in hiding at present, and I'll not reveal their locations unless ye do what I ask. If we complete this mission, I'll never have to work again. I'll buy a nice manor home and buy new clothes for all of ye. Just help me, Lewis, and if ye wish, I'll never speak with ye again. If ye dinnae help me, I'll be forced to sell them to an unsavory person. I have no choice. I am out of coin and canno' find work anywhere."

Lewis found the situation of being forced to sift through his sire's words to search for any truths to be difficult. What was the truth? Were the two still at the abbey or had they been dragged away?

"They are well hidden, Lewis. Ye'll never find them. If ye wish to see yer sisters again, ye'll do what I ask. One patrol and ye are free."

Lewis mulled over the situation, unable to tell what the lies were. He had no idea but he couldn't risk never seeing his sisters again. He didn't doubt that his father would have taken the girls back and found a place to hide them, nor did he doubt that he would sell them. The realization that his father would do anything for coin was something hard to accept. But for his sisters' sake, he had to.

Forced to go along with him, he gave his terms to the agreement. "If I do assist ye, ye'll allow the girls to come with me. I will help ye, but ye will no' ask my friends. They have to return to the clan or the Mathesons will send a search party out for us." He didn't know for certain that this would happen, but if Grif were gone for long, Isla's father would come looking for him, so in theory, it was true. "The girls dinnae belong with ye. They belong with other lasses their age. They need to learn how to read, how to sew. They can join Clan Matheson and live a life of a young lass, not a nun."

Stunned that the man could even consider selling his sisters at such a tender age, he had to fight not to choke the man standing in front of him. But after everything else he'd just learned about him, he had to consider the possibility that he would commit such an egregious act. Reeling and disgusted from this admission, he tried to think of just punishment for committing such a crime, but he couldn't. What if he were to take the man out of the inn and force him to show him where the girls were held? Then he could take them to Clan Matheson now.

"Oh, by the way. Have ye heard yet that the sheriffs are looking for a certain thief in Inverness?

His name is Lewis Haggert. If ye think to defy me, I'll report yer presence immediately."

He'd forgotten that. "Ye are scum, Da. Ye dinnae deserve to have bairns."

"I never wanted ye anyway. I punched yer mother in the belly twice to get rid of ye, but ye were a tough one."

His poor mother. He wondered how she had survived living with the man for so long.

"I see ye are thinking hard. Think on this. Yer sisters are young and untouched. They'll get me good coin, so if ye dinnae help me, I'll be selling them soon. I'll have no trouble selling the lasses at their age. Men like them young."

Lewis lost all control. He grabbed his father and threw him against the wall, choking him. "Ye foul bastard. Sell yer own daughters to be raped? What kind of man does that?"

"A man who never wanted any of ye to begin with," his sire said through clenched teeth. "Leave me be. Send yer friends away now, and ye'll stay where I can hear ye. Ye'll no' be telling them any of what we planned."

The door flew open, and Grif entered, grabbing Lewis and setting him back in the chair. "He's no' worth it, Haggert."

Lewis knew Grif was right. "My thanks to ye." He brushed his hands of the filth he'd touched, then said. "Listen, I'm going to stay a few more days with my sire. Ye and Steinn head home on the morrow. I'll see ye after Yule." He needed Grif to go back and get help. Find some Matheson guards to assist him. Asking Grif and Steinn to stay and help him against a score or more would be guaranteeing they'd all be hurt. Three of them would not be enough to take care of his father and his men. So he had to get Grif to go back and get help. And he needed to make his sire believe he would help them so he could learn the location of his sisters.

He had to save them. He wouldn't go back to Black Isle without them.

The only problem was how to tell Grif that he needed more Matheson guards. His father kept a keen eye on him, so there was no possible way he could just tell him to gather men and return.

Then a thought occurred to him, one that would surely bring a slew of men back to Inverness.

Grif scowled and questioned his move, something he'd expected. "Are ye sure about that? I can stay longer."

"Nay. Go back. Tell Shaw that I'll be back to join the guards after Yule. If they still allow me on the patrol, I'll do that too. After Yule." He calmed himself down and clasped his friend's shoulder. "I'll be fine and tell Ysenda that I love her."

Grif arched a brow at him, so he grinned and pushed him out the door.

"Happy Yuletide to ye and Isla," Lewis added.

Lewis had no idea how many men were in this group of his father's, but he guessed that the three of them could not fight off however many men it took to overtake a nobleman carrying coin with numerous guards. He would need help and lots of it. Since his father had the girls hidden somewhere, he had no choice in the matter. He'd have to stay and do what his father demanded to protect his dear sisters.

He would do this one thing for his father, then he would gather his sisters and bring them to Matheson land.

As long as no sheriffs discovered his name, he'd be safe. But would his own father turn him in?

He had to pray he would not.

⚬

Ysenda woke up in the middle of the night, visions of white teeth trying to bite her in the neck fresh in her mind. Why wouldn't the nightmares stop?

It seemed she'd had them more frequently ever since she'd hurt her leg, and she had no idea why. She'd also had an odd dream about Lewis. He was wandering through the forest, lost, and couldn't find anyone to help him.

She found her walking stick and made her way out the door to the courtyard, feeling the express need for fresh air. She'd left her contraption on at night because it needed two people to arrange it properly. After so many weeks in confinement, she was desperate for space and the fresh, crisp air of the Highlands. It kept her awake.

No one was about, so she made her way across the courtyard as carefully as she could. It was time to visit the horses. Ethan was out rubbing down his horse, humming quietly, a tune that soothed all the beasts. He was usually up until midnight, since he didn't require as much sleep as many.

"Another nightmare, lass?" he asked as soon as she entered.

"Aye. I needed fresh air and the smell of a horse. Any horse."

"The one ye rode is here. She's a sweet mare." He pointed to two stalls down from the one he was in.

Ysenda made her way down to the horse, surprised that the mare knickered at her presence. She leaned into her and whispered, "Ye remember me, aye? I'm glad ye were no' hurt in my fall."

Ethan tossed her an apple, and she held the treat for the animal, the sound of the chomping calming her insides. There was something soothing about the life in a stable. Ethan stopped and turned toward the door.

"What is it?" she asked.

"Hoofbeats. Two horses arriving."

"Grif and Lewis mayhap?"

He looked out and replied, "I'll check because the gate is closed. Ye stay here. I'm going on the curtain wall."

Ysenda made her way over to the doorway and waited, not surprised to see Ethan opening the gate with one of the guards after coming down from the wall. In came Grif and Steinn. She looked past them, expecting to see Lewis, but he was not there.

The two brought their horses to the stable and dismounted, leading their animals inside into the warmth of the building. Ysenda stood off to the side, wondering what had happened to Lewis, but the riders said nothing, brushing their horses down first after giving them each a small bucket of oats.

She waited as patiently as she could, finally speaking up once they finished with their horses. "Where is he?" she blurted out.

Grif spun around and said, "Ye mean Lewis? He met up with his sire and decided to stay with him. Told us to leave him there. Said he would see us after Yule."

Ysenda frowned. "I dinnae like the sound of that."

Steinn said, "Neither did we, but he insisted."

"He hates his sire. Why would he stay?"

"Och, and he sent a message for ye, Ysenda." Grif gained a wide grin on his face. "He said to tell ye that he loves ye."

"What?" She thought for a moment and recalled the night they'd both been in their cups. Right before Aunt Brigid and Uncle Marcas had come inside. He'd made an odd comment to her. Then she recalled it exactly. "That is no' good news."

"Why no'? I thought ye liked him," Grif replied, looking at her oddly.

"Ye dinnae understand. Lewis told me that if he ever sent a message that he loved me that there would be something wrong." That was it. "We canno' ignore the message. He needs help."

She was certain of it.

"What are ye talking about?" Grif asked, walking closer to her.

She repeated what she recalled of their

interaction to Grif, word for word. "'Tis what he said. Where was he when he said that to ye?"

Steinn said, "She could be right, Grif. His sire was right behind him when he said that to us. Do ye think he was using trickery or something to make him stay?"

"Or make him do something like steal for him?" Grif said, his eyes wide. "That could be it. But I dinnae believe he would do it for his sire. He hates him, and they were no' the least bit friendly. In fact, I pulled him off his father when I went in the room. He had his sire against the wall, choking him. His sire was laughing."

"His sisters," Ysenda said, chewing on a fingernail. "What if he threatened to hurt his sisters? Would he do whatever he asked to save his sisters?"

"Aye," Ethan said, coming in behind her. "I overheard yer conversation. It makes perfect sense to me that Lewis' father is blackmailing him into committing some crime. 'Tis why he sent ye away and why he gave ye the message for Ysenda. He knew she would remember what he said."

"Shite," Grif muttered, his hand on his hips.

"Hellfire," Steinn said, tossing his brush down on the ground. "Why did we no' think of that, Grif?"

"Because the message was for Ysenda. He knew we wouldn't figure it out until he was gone. We have to go back." Grif paced in the small area. "I know no' where we'll find him, but we have to go back."

"I'm sure they were no' going far or he would

have let us know that somehow. I say we return to the last place we saw him," Steinn said.

Ethan said, "I'll tell Marcas we need a group to leave on the morrow at first light.

"We go now," Ysenda said.

"Hellfire, ye canno' go, lass. Are ye daft?" Grif asked.

"I'm fine. I can ride a horse. I just need help mounting and dismounting."

Ethan looked at her and then said to Grif, "She's been walking with that new contraption, and she's been careful. Jennet said it has been nearly a moon and a half. She's nearly healed. I'll send two guards with ye now, and we'll follow with a few more on the morrow. But ye must agree to help her mount and dismount."

"We agree, but can I no' sleep for a couple of hours, Ysenda?"

Ethan nodded. "Aye, give him that much, lass. I'll have the men ready in two hours. Ye need to pack yer saddlebag and find food. Their horses need a rest too."

Ysenda grumbled a bit, but then she looked at how tired Steinn was, his eyelids drooping. "Go ahead. I'll wake ye when I'm ready."

"Two hours, please?" Steinn begged.

"Aye. Two hours. Then we're going to find Lewis, and we're no' returning without him."

CHAPTER TWENTY-ONE

LEWIS STOOD WITH the group of bandits in the forest. Hiding.

A group of grown men hiding. He felt ridiculous.

His father couldn't stop talking. The man was actually excited about the prospect of attacking and stealing from a nobleman. "I promise ye this will be a worthwhile attack. I've heard the amount of gold coins they'll be carrying will weigh the horses down. They have extra horses for that reason."

The leader of the group went by Albert. He stood taller than everyone but Lewis and had a long, black beard and no front teeth.

"They should be here soon, right, Albert?" one of the others asked.

"Within the hour. Aye. Just relax."

Lewis stood as far away from his father as he could. He hated the bastard. His mind went to Ysenda, and he couldn't help but wonder if she would recall the exact words he'd said when they were both in their cups. Would she remember what he had said if she ever heard that phrase again? Would she recognize it meant he was in trouble?

He prayed she would.

And if not, he prayed that Grif and Steinn suspected enough to get some Matheson guards to come back and get him. He did not wish to be killed by any of the men who would be coming along to protect the earl they planned to attack. Or was it a marquess?

He had to hope that the nobleman's group would outnumber his sire's group. And once they were defeated, Lewis would take his leave. He would not attack anyone so he should be free to go whenever he wished.

How he prayed they would see it the same as he did.

The sound of hoofbeats caught him, sending his blood into a wild current racing through his insides. He froze, waiting to see who would arrive.

In truth, he hadn't decided exactly what he was going to do. His instructions had been simple. Protect them from the earl's guards. From what he knew of those type of guards, they did not attack people. It was their job to protect the earl and anyone else on the trip with them. So, they tighten in a group, probably around the one who carried the gold coins. Their job was to make it difficult for anyone to ride by and grab the valuable coins.

They would not be attacking his father or the men with him, but they could kill to defend the earl and his coin.

His father's cronies would be on the attack,

and he had vowed to his core that he would not involve himself in that. He was not going to attack anyone, nor would he kill anyone for fear of being caught and hung by the roadside.

His sire had surely turned daft.

He hid in the trees, away from the rest of the band of thieves. Just before the approaching group broke into their view, his sire whispered, "Ye better protect me. Dinnae think hiding in the trees will save yer sisters. I need this coin."

"So ye can gamble it away?" he drawled.

His father tried to hit him, but he was far enough away. The man was surely a fool. Did he not realize how much stronger and more powerful his son was? Apparently not, or his sire would not have talked to him the way he did.

Lewis knew one thing for sure. If the opportunity arose, he'd put his sword through his sire's belly before he'd ever directly attack an earl.

The horses came around the bend, surprising him by their number. And the man in the center appeared to be of noble blood. His boots looked to be of the finest leather, and they shined as if they'd been fussed over for hours. But it was the gloves the man wore, the gold embroidery something he'd never seen. It had to be something only the wealthy could afford. The gloves and the two heavy bags on either side of his horse told him that the group was the one they'd waited for. The bags were so heavy that the poor horse was nearly foaming from the heavy load.

There were seven men around the earl, and all carried small swords like the English did. He saw no quivers or evidence of any archers. Albert let out a shrill whistle, and the men came out of the forest, ten of them including his sire, and they stopped in front of the group.

Albert halted near the first horse. "We'll take that bag on the side of the horse. Ye can even keep the other one. Share the wealth and we'll go on our way."

The man in front chuckled and said, "Ye have to get it yerself, and I dinnae think ye can."

To his surprise, Albert whistled, and the skirmish began, a melee of swinging swords flashing through the air as Albert's group attacked the men in the circle who kept the earl inside a tight loop.

His sire called out, "Get yer arse out here, son!"

Lewis wouldn't move. He watched the chaos as swords swung, men flew off horses, and the skirmish spread wider. His father struck one man's arm and knocked his weapon onto the ground, and then he raised his arm in celebration.

Another came at his sire, but he fought him off.

What he saw next nearly caused him to fall off his horse.

But he hung on because he had to help her.

Her!

His eyes deceived him at first, but he waited, unable to believe what his eyes told him. Coming toward him were Grif, Steinn, two Matheson guards, and hellfire if his eyes did not deceive him. Ysenda rode a horse with that odd contraption still on her leg.

He'd kill Grif for bringing her along, though

he knew her well enough to know how stubborn she was. Either way, he had to go assist her. There was no way he'd allow her to ride into the melee. She needed to be in a tree, well-hidden, and able to use her arrow.

He headed in her direction, but he cursed because he hadn't been quick enough in his decision. To his dismay, something happened that sent him flying out of the forest.

Another horse knocked into hers and she did what he feared would take place, the one thing that would put her over the edge.

She fell off her horse.

***

Ysenda landed hard on her arse. Frozen at first, she didn't know what to do as she watched her mount run away from the crowd.

And her.

Her quiver and bow in her hand still, she rolled onto her side, trying her best to get up with the blasted contraption on her leg. Grif and Steinn were in the middle of the melee, and fortunately, she was still a distance away from the fight.

She didn't see Lewis anywhere, though she would have guessed that Grif might have seen him and motioned for her or Steinn to get involved. There was clearly a nobleman in the middle, protecting whatever he had brought along with him. Surrounded by a circle of swordsmen, they fought a group of reivers, rough and ruthless. The clash of weaponry and the screams of pain told her how hard the group battled. Grif would know

Lewis' sire, so perhaps that was why he jumped so quickly into the chaos.

Finally able to sit up, Ysenda vowed to get to her feet and out of the way, but a horse headed directly toward her.

A vision of some type of beast with pointed teeth came to her. She shook her head to banish the image from her mind, but it wouldn't leave her, instead the sudden fear of a boar biting her neck overtook her until she screamed.

Lewis bellowed at her. "Get up, and I'll get ye!"

She heard his voice and searched for him but couldn't find him anywhere. All she saw was a jaw full of teeth.

"Ysenda, I'll not let the beast get ye. Look at me!"

Through her tears, she finally managed to find his face—his gorgeous face with the loving eyes—and she clung to that image instead. He reached down and pulled her to her feet, shouting at her, "What the hell are ye doing here? Ye dinnae belong here with yer leg."

Lifting her onto his lap, still on horseback, he headed straight for a tree in the forest off to the side of the main path.

"Ye said ye loved me. I knew that meant ye were in trouble, so stop yelling at me." She glanced over her shoulder at him and said, "Did ye think we would no' come if ye said ye were in trouble? And so ye are aware, my leg is nearly healed. Aunt Brenna said so."

"Did ye happen to think that mayhap I do love ye, and it was no' meant to bring ye here?"

"Well, if ye do, ye should say so!" Her voice came out in a shout, to her surprise.

"Well, I do love ye. What do ye think of that?"

Stunned by his answer, she stared straight ahead and mumbled. "I like it."

"What?"

"I said I like it." Where was that shouting voice of hers again?

"Canno' hear ye, lass."

She whirled her head to look at him and exclaimed, "Mayhap I love ye too."

"'Tis a fine thing to say," he barked. "Then get yer arse in that tree where ye belong so ye live long enough for me to court ye. Ye still have a broken leg or have ye forgotten?"

She broke into laughter and replied, "Fine with me. I prefer the tree whether my leg is broken or no'."

He found a perfect tree and lifted her up to a branch that she could settle in.

"Are ye set? Because there are more reivers than the earl has guards. We need yer help."

"I'm set."

"Good," he growled as he took off toward the skirmish. He turned around and winked at her, a wide smile on his face. "Now shoot the reivers. They're trying to rob innocent people."

How could she fall in love with anyone but Lewis? She loved the way they bantered back and forth. She just wasn't the type of lass to look at a man and whimper with the words of love and adoration. Shouting at each other was much more their style.

Taking a good look at the group in front of her, she nocked an arrow and fired. The reivers were now fighting a losing battle since the five Matheson guards had come to the nobleman's aid. She wondered which one was his father, thinking she should leave him be, but she had no idea until she watched one man try to pull Lewis off his horse.

"Ye're killing the wrong men. Ye are supposed to be defending me!" the man yelled at Lewis.

"I dinnae protect thieves!" Lewis said. Rather than hurt his own father, if she were to guess, he moved his horse away from that man and went after a man with a long beard.

Ysenda nocked an arrow and let it fly, catching the bearded man in the chest just as Lewis reached him. He fell off his horse, and Lewis turned around to grin at her, nodding his head in gratitude.

She fired two more, catching one reiver in the back and another in his thigh. The thieving group was clearly losing. In fact, some of the men protecting the nobleman in the center had stopped fighting because there were no more men coming toward them. One of the attackers fell off his horse and ran. Two other reivers turned tail and headed back into the forest.

Grif approached Lewis while Steinn spoke to the man in the middle. It appeared that the fight was over, so Ysenda stopped nocking and waited to see what would happen next.

She had to love Lewis. Who else would see

her on the ground and remember her fear? He had come to her, yelling at her exactly what she needed to hear to pull her out of the trance that was overpowering her.

And she wasn't in any hurry to climb down out of the tree either. In fact, she made the decision to wait until Lewis came back for her.

The sudden interruption made her realize she'd made the right decision. Two deer came out of the woods and ran across the clearing, totally unaware of the number of hunters about. Two Matheson guards moved quickly to stop the animals, but Ysenda knew they'd probably never move close enough to the stag to use their swords, so she nocked an arrow, waited until just the right moment, then let the arrow fly across the land, hitting it in its flank. A cheer went up among the men as they closed in on the animal, knowing that they could get it back to Matheson land in this cold. The deer would make fine stew for the upcoming holiday. She smiled as the men surrounded the one animal, the other one long gone.

But then something caught her eye. His father, she assumed it was him, came sneaking out of the forest straight toward the group, catching the men completely unaware.

This time, he moved his horse slowly toward Lewis.

Lewis was now abreast of Grif and Steinn, all talking with the men guarding the deer in the center.

"Lewis! Watch yer back!" She had the oddest feeling that the man, who she thought was his father, was going straight for Lewis. To talk with him? They were in the worst spot because she didn't have a clear view from the tree she was in.

Lewis couldn't hear her. The men were all talking and laughing enough that no one heard her. And no one noticed the man on horseback. What if he was going after Lewis?

She dropped down out of the tree as carefully as she could, doing her best to ignore the vision that threatened to overtake her as soon as her feet hit the ground, her head jerking to the side because the image of a running boar came to her.

She forced herself to ignore it, her heart beating so fast that her vision blurred.

But the man now held his sword over his head, doing his best to sneak up behind Lewis.

Tears blurred her vision as the growl of the boar met her ear, but she told herself it wasn't there. She had to save Lewis. She nocked her arrow, sweat threatening to drip into her eyes as she did it, and the boar now racing straight at her.

She let the arrow fly and hit his father in the back, even as his sword arm was nearly over Lewis' head. The man pitched forward in his saddle, his sword dropping to the ground and missing all the men.

Lewis and Grif spun around, their faces shocked by this turn of events. Lewis caught the man before he fell off his horse, then he saw the arrow in his back and his weapon on the ground. His gaze searched behind him, first to the tree where she'd been but then to her.

Just before the boar caught her, her scream ripping through the air.

CHAPTER TWENTY-TWO

L EWIS GOT TO her so quickly that she was still screaming. "I have ye. Ye are fine, Ysenda. There are no beasts here." He jumped down from his horse and tugged her close, wrapping his arms around her while he guarded her leg.

He scoured her clothing for any sign of blood in case she'd been struck by a sword or a thrown dagger, but he saw no wounds anywhere.

"Is it the boar? 'Tis why ye scream so?" He sat down, settling her on his lap. There were no more villains around, so he knew they were safe. Cuddling her close, he wished to banish whatever was in her mind. "Ysenda, talk to me. Tell me why ye cry so."

She slowed her sobs, stopping to allow her gaze to search the area after looking up at him.

He declared, "I knew I should never have told ye I loved ye. 'Tis why ye are crying, is it no'? Ye dinnae return my love and so ye hate me."

That brought a giggle bubbling from her chest, and she smiled at him, her breath still hitching.

"Ye hate me. I knew it." He rolled his eyes skyward and clutched his hand to his heart.

"Nay," she managed to get out between hiccups. "I love ye too." She peeked over his shoulder. "This was the worst one yet. I swear the boar was coming for me. I saw him jump. Lewis, I'm losing my mind. What will I do? Am I turning daft?"

"Nay, ye arenae daft. Ye have just been under a little bit of pressure. An avalanche, a broken leg, a bunch of reivers. Just yer usual occurrences."

She repositioned herself, wiping her tears. "I am fine. Did ye find my sweet mare? She ran off."

"I think she's waiting for ye over there, munching on some grass." He tipped his head toward the opposite side of the road.

There she was, oblivious to all the sounds around her.

"Come, we must get up. Someone is coming this way." He nodded toward the bend and at a group of three horses headed toward the group.

Lewis stood and lifted her up, whistling to draw her horse over. Pleased to see the beast come quickly, he lifted her onto the mare's back, then mounted his own horse.

The visitors were three sheriffs. He was shocked to see they'd come along to protect the earl. The nobleman spoke to them, updating them on what had happened.

The sheriff in the middle announced, "We're looking for someone named Haggert."

Lewis thought he might heave into the corner. What did they want with him? "My name is Haggert. What do ye want with me?"

The sheriff looked at him as he approached on his horse, while Ysenda remained behind him. Lewis thought his free days were probably over. His sire had given his name to some people as "Lewis Haggert" instead of his true name of "Goerge," so he was probably about to be arrested for his sire's crimes. What defense would he have against his father's lies?

"We're looking for Goerge Haggert. He's much older than ye. Wanted for thievery."

Lewis let out a sigh of relief. Grif said, "That bastard is on the ground with an arrow in his back."

As if on cue, his sire let out a groan.

Lewis said, "He lives."

Two sheriffs dismounted and made their way over to him. One pulled out the arrow and rolled him over onto his back. "Goerge Haggert?"

"Aye?" He opened his eyes and finally determined that it was a sheriff questioning him. "What? Not me. Ye want my son. He's the guilty one."

"Aye, we heard all those stories. We've got four complaints against ye, Haggert. And we were already warned that ye would try to accuse yer son of yer nasty deeds. Ye're going away for a long time."

They dragged his father to his feet and then threw him on a horse, after binding his hands. He never stopped yelling. "I'm injured. These men should be arrested. Arrest my son. 'Tis his fault."

"Shut up. Save it for the judge." The middle

sheriff was not about to listen to his father's lies, fortunately. "Ye need any help, Earl?"

"Nay, we'll be on our way thanks to the help of these men."

A sudden thought occurred to Lewis and he bellowed, "Wait!"

"What is it?" one sheriff asked.

"I need to ask him a question. He said he had my sisters hidden away. I need to know where."

His father laughed. "Ye think I'll tell ye now? Ye'll never find out."

One of the sheriffs, an incredulous expression on his face, looked to Lewis and asked, "He hid yer sisters on ye and ye have no idea where they are?"

Lewis nodded, so angry that he feared speaking.

The sheriff knocked him off the horse. "I guess ye'll be walking."

"Ye canno' make me walk. 'Tis cruel."

The second sheriff said, "Nay, 'tis cruel to hide two lasses. How old are they?"

"Ten and twelve," Grif replied, clasping Lewis' shoulder in a show of support.

The sheriff pointed to his father's feet and said, "Take yer boots off."

"What?" his father asked, wide-eyed. "Why?"

"Because ye are cruel to two innocent lasses. Unless ye wish to tell the truth. If ye dinnae, yer walking barefoot. We should be there by the morrow."

His father looked from one sheriff to the next, all three crossing their arms. He finally conceded.

"They're still at the abbey. I never took them," he mumbled.

"Ye lied to yer son?"

He shrugged his shoulders and said, "He deserved it."

The third sheriff punched the old man, then tossed him over the horse. "If he's lying, come tell us. We'll make him pay."

With that, his father was gone, taken away by three men of the law. His judgment day had finally arrived. Lewis had an odd feeling of nostalgia course through him as he watched the man who raised him taken away, but then he thought of how long the bastard had let Lewis believe that he'd been accused of thievery by the chieftain of Clan Ross. That nostalgia turned into relief quickly.

Reminding himself that the cruel bastard had tried to blame his dear sister, he knew this was what needed to happen. His father would not stop terrorizing everyone he knew. This was justice. Finally.

Grif said, "'Tis what he deserves, Lewis."

"I know. It just feels odd to think of him in prison, even though I know it's where he belongs."

The earl said, "Men like that never change, son. Ye've chosen the right way. Be proud of yerself."

"Many thanks, my lord," he mumbled, not knowing exactly how to speak to an earl.

The nobleman said, "I believe ye each deserve a small piece of my wealth. If not for yer assistance, I would have lost half of it."

He reached into the bag and pulled out several

shiny gold coins. After the earl gave them each a small reward, they took their leave.

Grif said, "Ye ready to go home? Ye are hale, Ysenda?"

"I'm fine. Stupid boar again. Forgive me."

Grif chuckled. "Naught to forgive. I'll thank ye instead for keeping my friend from having his head cleaved in two by his own sire."

"Nice shot," Steinn said. "Hell, but I wish I could shoot like that."

Lewis said to the group, "I only have one more request. Would ye mind if we took a detour to the abbey? I'd like to bring my sisters back to Matheson land for Yule."

"I hope they are returning forever," Steinn said.

Ysenda waited when they approached the abbey. On the way, Lewis had told her all about his sisters and how they'd been left at the abbey. When they approached the front gate, Lewis said, "I'm here to see my sisters."

"Nae sisters here. Go on yer way."

Lewis stepped up to the man at the gate and said, "I was here before, and I spoke to one of yer men. He lied to me just as ye just did. Now, do ye wish to continue lying or shall I hang ye from the parapets as I did with him?"

The man paled but lifted his chin a notch in defiance. "Not here."

Lewis grabbed the fool's neck and lifted him off the ground. "I didnae hear ye correctly."

"Aye," he managed to get out. "Aye. One moment, please."

Lewis set him down and said, "My thanks to ye. I'm here to pick them up. Ready them for me, if ye please."

The man glared at him, but then hurried away from the gates.

"Are ye sure he'll return?" Ysenda whispered.

Steinn chuckled. "If ye'd seen how he scared the other man, ye wouldnae ask. I'm sure they all remember us."

It wasn't long before two lasses raced straight for Lewis, launching themselves at him.

"Truly?" one asked. "Ye are taking us away from this horrid place?"

"Aye," he said hugging the first one while the other stopped and burst into tears.

"Come, Elspeth. Meet my friends. We are here to escort ye to yer new home."

"Ye will live with us, Lewis?" Elspeth mumbled between sobs.

"Aye. I'll have to go hunting or patrolling since I'm a guard, but 'tis where I plan to live. Come. Meet my friends."

Elspeth came forward and squeezed her brother so hard that Ysenda nearly broke into tears while she watched them. Lewis was a good brother. He obviously loved his sisters dearly, and they adored him. He had a big heart, something she loved about him. He loved with all his heart.

Finella said, "Take us home quickly. Please Lewis. I fear they'll make us return."

He led them out the gate and over to their horses,

stopping to introduce the lasses to everyone, but he stopped and moved over to Ysenda on her horse. "Finella, Elspeth, this is Ysenda, and I plan to court her when we return. That is, if her sire gives me permission."

"Ye might marry, Lewis?" Elspeth asked with a squeal.

"We might. Only time will tell," he replied.

Finella asked, "Ye will be our sister?"

Ysenda glanced first at Lewis, his eyes so full of love that she wished to cry with his sisters. "Aye, mayhap someday." Then she decided to say something to stop the tears. "But only if he promises not to be mean to me. Ye know he likes to tease me."

Finella's laughter could be heard on Ramsay land, or so Ysenda thought. "He likes to tease us too."

And Ysenda fell in love with Finella and Elspeth on the spot.

CHAPTER TWENTY-THREE

THE GROUP GATHERED in the great hall after the midday meal the next day, everyone anxious to hear the story of the big battle. Ysenda had already had her leg checked out and was pleased that she hadn't done any damage. Elspeth and Finella had been welcomed with open arms and were presently with Charlotte fixing the chamber up for the new members of the clan. Ysenda's grandfather was there, of course, along with her grandmother, her parents, Torrian and Nellie, and also Brigid and Marcas.

She let Lewis tell the story because he was the only one who knew all the parts about his father's threats against his sisters and about the group's plan to attack the earl for his gold coins, as well how Ysenda had saved Lewis from his own father before his arrest.

When Lewis ended the tale, he said, "It was quite a skirmish, but the earl offered each of us a few coins for our assistance."

"He should have. They could have lost all," her grandfather said. "Ye had good timing."

"But now, I have something else I wish to say."

Ysenda whirled around because she had no idea what he was alluding to. What did he have to say to her family that he hadn't already said? She narrowed her gaze at him and he winked at her with a smile.

"I'm listening," her grandsire said, though she threw him one quick glare.

"We're all listening. Ignore my sire," her father said, also tossing a glare at her grandfather, who snorted.

"While I'd like to tell ye about my feelings for yer daughter and granddaughter, Ysenda, I could tell ye that she is temperamental, stubborn, impulsive, foolish, and emotional…"

Ysenda nearly gasped enough for everyone to hear her, but she thought she contained herself. What was wrong with him? She wasn't temperamental, was she? True about being stubborn and emotional—she nearly cried just meeting his sisters—how could he say she was foolish? It took all she had not to turn around and leave the hall.

"But I shan't. Instead I'll tell ye that I've gotten to know her verra well lately. After all, we survived an avalanche, a snowstorm, the next morn after our encounter with the finest *breath of life* ever made, and an attack by sheriffs and a stag, all while we were together. During all that time, I've learned much about her."

"Stubborn, foolish," her grandfather recited. "Get on with yer words, Haggert."

"Nay, none of those. Instead I'll tell ye that I've learned to admire her patience, her strength during adversity, her big heart, her intelligence, and the ability to fire an arrow unlike any other."

Ysenda's shock at his words was the only thing that prevented the tears from flooding her cheeks.

He took her hand and led her over to stand in front of her parents and her grandparents. "I request permission to announce our betrothal to be at some later date, giving me the chance to court yer daughter as she wishes. I pledge to honor her and protect her with my life if ye will allow this betrothal."

"Do ye love her?" her mother asked.

"With every part of my being. I love her heart, her sassy nature, and her quick wit. And I pray someday she will love me the same."

That part did her in. The tears fell and she was powerless to stop them. With all his teasing and jesting, this was the most serious she'd ever seen him and she loved it. Staring at her sire between her tears, she caught the wide grin that crossed his face as he looked down at her and said, "He knows ye well, daughter. Even the sassiness."

Her mother nodded and her father said, "Ye have our permission."

Her grandfather said, "Are ye no' going to ask me, Gavin?"

"Nay." Her father shook his head. "I know yer feelings, Da. Ye've told me many times he'd be a good man once he settled. He's settled."

"Many thanks to ye," Lewis said to her father, then he leaned down to give her a quick kiss on her lips. Then he whispered, "Will ye marry me, Ysenda?"

She wrapped her arms around his neck and hugged him tight, barely able to get her words out. "Aye."

A bustle of congratulations took up the next few moments but then Torrian's voice carried over the group. "I have something I'd like to ask."

Ysenda had no idea what he was about, so she turned to give their chieftain her full attention.

Torrian stepped closer. "I'd like to ask ye a question, Ysenda. Because I heard rumblings about it, but Lewis didnae mention it. I'd like the truth of it."

"Of course, ask me whatever ye like," she said.

"Ye thought there was a boar in the woods? Is that why ye screamed at the end?"

"Aye," she said, a bit embarrassed to admit the truth of the situation. "I thought one came out of the woods and was headed straight for me. I could see him out of the corner of my eye."

"Yet ye still struck the man with a perfect shot," her grandfather said, an expression of pride evident on his face.

"She sure did," Lewis said. "I was stunned, but I was more stunned that after she let the arrow fly, she fell to the ground wrestling with an invisible monster, screaming as though she were dying. Thank goodness when I reached her that she grabbed onto me and stopped."

"And there was nothing there?" Aunt Brigid asked. "What an amazing testament to yer core, lass."

All was quiet until Ysenda mumbled, "I wish I understood it, but I dinnae."

Torrian stood and moved over to stand in front of her grandfather. "Uncle Logan, 'tis time. Ye tell her now or I will."

"Torrian, there's no reason to upset the lass any more than she is. Leave it be."

Her grandmother's voice carried from across the room. "Logan Ramsay, ye better do what yer chieftain tells ye. If no', I'll come over there and make ye tell all."

That comment would have made many chuckle, but no one laughed this time.

And that included her grandmother.

Ysenda couldn't figure out exactly what was going on. What the hell were they talking about? What did Torrian wish for her grandfather to say? She had to know.

She stood and strode over to stand in front of her grandsire. "Grandda? What is he talking about?" Visions of a young Torrian and a younger grandfather began to pop in and out of her mind.

Torrian with an arrow.

Her grandfather knocking her down.

A pony next to them.

A boar looking directly at her. But one not moving.

Dead?

Her grandfather lying across her so much that she couldn't breathe.

"Grandda?" she asked again, tears misting her vision.

"Now, Uncle Logan. Can ye not see the way the poor lass twitches? She's fighting the memories now." Torrian moved closer, his arms crossed in front of him.

Her grandfather stood up and barked, "Fine. I will tell all of ye, but ye are to keep yer comments and questions to yerselves until I finish. I had my reasons, and ye dinnae need to know them. But she does need to hear this. Gavin, I will speak with ye later. And ye too, Gwynie." His bark came out so abrupt that no one said a word, everyone staying seated, while waiting to hear what he had to say.

Lewis came up behind her and wrapped his arms around her.

"Sit her down, Haggert. She needs to be seated."

Lewis led her back to a chair by the hearth, turning her to face her grandfather. All eyes were on the man, the one everyone looked to for guidance.

What the hell had happened?

Her grandfather approached, close enough that she noticed the clench in his jaw, the tension in his fists, and if she were to guess, she thought he was about to cry. She nearly got up, but Lewis tugged her lightly and rubbed her arm as if to tell her to let it be for now.

The elder of the clan paced a bit then stopped in front of her. "Ye were three. I'd promised ye a ride on the pony, so we went out to the stables. Ye chose yer pony, and I set ye on his back and led him all around the courtyard. But being the headstrong lass that ye are, being Gwynie's and my granddaughter, that wasnae enough for ye. Ye wished to go out into the meadow, into the forest,

all the way to Grant land to see Uncle Alex, so
ye told me.

"So I took ye outside the gates. We were nearly
at the forest when Torrian called out to me. We
had an issue where he was sending an army of
guards out, so the men had been called off the
curtain wall to prepare. He wanted my opinion
about something, so I stopped the pony and gave
him my full attention.

"That was my mistake. Ye climbed down off
the pony and headed straight for the forest. By
the time Torrian and I noticed ye were off the
pony, ye were halfway to the woods. A boar came
flying out headed straight for ye, and ye giggled,
shouting, 'Doggie.'

"My heart was in my throat. We both raced
after ye, calling ye back, but ye were laughing and
running, ignoring both of us. Why ye werenae
afraid of the beast, I'll never know, but ye ran
straight at him. Torrian held back to nock an
arrow, but I dove when he was nearly upon ye,
knocking ye to the side. I rolled on ye to protect
ye from his bite just as Torrian's arrow hit the
boar in the neck, and I plunged my dagger into
its belly a moment later."

Small gasps escaped from a few, but no one said
anything.

"When I dared to look at ye, ye were staring
right into the beast's face, and even though his
jaw was still open, ye were scowling at him. I got
up, picked ye up, carried ye back inside the keep,
and I made Torrian promise no' to tell anyone. I
will admit that it was the worst moment of my

life. I'll never forget it. The memory of it has haunted me many times too."

All were silent and Gwynie stood up. Grandda held his hand up and said, "Before ye all yell at me and ask me why I kept it a secret, I'll tell ye why. Ye know what our bairns and grandbairns mean to me. If Merewen had learned the truth, would she ever have allowed Ysenda to be in my care again? Would ye, Gavin? Brigid? Would ye have allowed me to be alone with Reyna? Brenna, would ye have allowed me to be alone with Bethia's bairns or Gregor's? Hell nay, and I wouldnae blame ye. I counted on the fact that she was too young to recall it. She wasnae talking much either, so I didnae worry about her telling anyone. 'Twas a risk I was willing to take. I had no idea it would come back to haunt her when she was two decades older."

Then he did the one thing she'd never seen before. Tears blurred his vision, but before everyone else noticed, he left the hall and went outside.

Before he made it to the door, Aunt Brenna called out to him. "Aye, Logan. I would trust ye with any of our bairns. What ye did was proof of the truth of yer heart."

Ysenda took Lewis' hand, set it aside, and said, "I'll be right back."

Her grandfather was headed straight for the stables, but she limped along, calling out to him, though she knew him well enough to know he wouldn't stop until he was ready to.

"Grandda!" She followed him to an apple tree

just inside the curtain wall, a deserted area where no one could see him.

He turned around to face her and said, "My apologies, lassie. I did no' intend any harm because of my foolishness."

She stood on the tiptoes of one foot and kissed his cheek. "I will always trust ye, Grandda. I love ye, and I know ye love me."

He wrapped his arms around her and did the one thing she hadn't expected.

The old warrior rested his head on her shoulder and sobbed.

EPILOGUE

YULE HAD STARTED that day, and everyone was cheerful. Ysenda finally had her contraption off her leg, though she still moved slowly. Elspeth and Finella had never been happier, and the hall was being decorated with the sweet smell of pine boughs and berries everywhere.

And her recurring nightmares had ended.

Lewis and Ysenda both joined the hunting group, wagers flying over who would get the greatest catch for the table. Some wished for venison while others hoped for boar or pheasant. They rode together away from the main group.

Ysenda said, "I think this is where we'll find a nice pheasant. We have to have at least one goose or pheasant. Mama and Papa will catch a big, fat boar for Grandda, but I prefer a feathered option." Her gaze narrowed as she scanned the area for any animal movement. "We have to get the best. Better than Torrian or my sire, Lewis. We have to."

"I wish to beat Grif and Steinn. They think because they are brothers that they'll win. And

Isla refused to shoot this year. I love it. We'll win for certes," he exclaimed.

All had gone beautifully since they'd returned.

In fact, he and Ysenda had handfasted because they just couldn't keep themselves apart, even if she wasn't ready to marry yet.

"A pheasant! I saw it in the brush." She motioned to Lewis to slow down.

This was one of her strengths. She had the unusual ability to hear that bird as it rustled through the brush, that odd sound they made allowing her to hit the catch without destroying the best part of the meat.

"Hush. I hear two of them," she said.

"I hear it too," he whispered. "Ye shoot first, but I'm trying too. I can hear it, Ysenda. 'Tis right there. If ye dinnae get it, I will."

Neither one of them made a sound until she heard the rustling again, so she let her arrow fly, hitting the bird and causing it to drop out of the bushes and off to the side. "I got it! I see it, Lewis."

Lewis let his arrow fly and a second loud thwack sounded, causing another bird to land off to the side. "I got one too."

"Two? We have two pheasants? Mama will be so proud!" Ysenda said.

The two dismounted and moved over to the spot where the birds lay, and they picked them up before tying them to their horses.

Then they proceeded to do their favorite thing after a successful hunt. "Lass, the way ye nock yer arrow excites me. We need to find our spot."

"It was the way ye let yers fly with such power. Aye. Our spot. Find it quickly, Lewis."

Neither spoke as their mounts flew across the landscape until they found a deserted hut in the middle of Gallow Hill Woods. A totally empty place.

Except for the two of them.

He dismounted and caught her as she slid down. "Och, lass. I dinnae know if I can wait."

He kissed her hard on the mouth, and she moaned, their tongues dueling with a fury that took her breath away. "Lewis, ye do love me, do ye no'?"

"Of course I do. Would I chase ye all the way here? We had to handfast because I could no' stand to be apart from ye any longer." He tore at her clothing, tossing her tunic behind them as they made their way into the hut.

"Nay, ye dinnae love me at all."

"Ye are right, I dinnae love ye."

"Ye can kiss my arse, Lewis Haggert."

"Naught I would rather do at the moment, Ysenda Ramsay."

She tugged on his tunic and tossed it behind her and then pulled her leggings down. Her nudity went straight to his member as he dropped his plaid, proudly standing up to let her know how much he loved her.

"I see ye do indeed like me."

"Nay, I changed my mind."

"Prove it." She touched his member and squeezed as a tease to him. The two were both nude, their hands reaching and caressing each other's bodies, kissing, suckling, and licking each other until they fell onto the bed.

Lewis spread her legs, his fingers testing her first. "Ye are slick for me already."

Then he positioned his body over her and set himself at the edge of her entrance, teasing her by pulsing inside and then pulling out.

"Do ye want me, lassie?"

"Nay, ye know I dinnae." Her moans could not be contained because she needed him so badly.

"I think ye do."

"Nay. I have no need for ye to come inside me, to fill me up. To hit me hard until I scream yer name. I dinnae want ye at all," she said.

Odd how their banter even came to them when they made frantic love to each other, but she loved it.

"Ye are lying to me."

He pushed inside a wee bit more, and she gulped with a deep moan. "Oh, Lewis."

There was always that moment of no return, when she could no longer tell lies about how much she needed him, wanted him, loved him. How she adored this man.

He grabbed her hips and thrust inside her with one swift move, and she smiled. "Aye, just what I needed."

The two worked their rhythm into a frenzy until she screamed his name out, and he followed her, basking in their pleasure together.

This was indeed their best life.

The great hall bustled with activity. Laughter echoed off the rafters as the group shared all their experiences of the last year.

The door opened, and they all jumped in unison. Everyone was already inside, so they had no idea who it was.

Maitland and Maeve entered to a hall that filled with applause, and he leaned down to kiss his new bride as everyone cheered for them. Behind him came his brother and his wife, along with two laddies, Wiley and Quillan, the two who had been kidnapped but had managed to save themselves.

Lots of hugs and best wishes bounced around the hall while more food was brought out from the kitchens. Fruit pastries, nuts and berries, and meat pies were shared with the newcomers.

Much later that eve and after the wee ones had already found their beds, questions became more serious. They filled Maitland in on all that had happened with Goerge Haggert and also explained how Ysenda's nightmares had ended.

Logan said, "I know it was wrong, Maitland, but ye canno' change the past. What's done is done, and I learned a lesson from it."

It was his daughter Brigid who had sat quietly and observed all the chatter, and then finally shocked everyone with her question.

"Da, there is one thing I wish to ask ye, and I would like the truth."

Her father grinned and said, "Ask me whatever ye wish. I'll answer if I can."

Her mother came closer, her arms crossed in

front of her as she stared at her husband. "I wish to listen to this because I believe 'tis the same question I have, Logan."

"Ask away, Gwynie."

Mother and daughter looked at each other, but finally Brigid nodded to her mother, giving her the opportunity to ask first.

Her grandmother looked at her grandfather and asked, "How many other secrets are ye hiding, Logan?"

He couldn't hide the subtle grin that crossed his face, but he stood from his chair and moved over to his wife, wrapping his arms around her and kissing her cheek. Then he said, "Good eve to ye, Gwynie."

And he walked away, whistling.

THE END

http://www.keiramontclair.com

D EAR READER,
    Thank you for reading Ysenda's story. There are only two more planned for this series, bringing the total to eight when we are done. Thea's story will be next and the last one belongs to Alaric Grant.

Is the part about Logan a cliffhanger? Will he reveal more secrets?

Only Logan knows the answer to that question. He never tells me until he's ready. I'm sure that doesn't surprise anyone.

Happy reading!

Keira Montclair

NOVELS BY
KEIRA MONTCLAIR

HIGHLAND HUNTERS
THE SCOT'S CONFLICT
THE SCOT'S TRAITOR
THE SCOT'S PROTECTOR
THE SCOT'S VOW
THE SCOT'S DESTINY
THE SCOT'S WARNING

HIGHLAND HEALERS
THE CURSE OF BLACK ISLE
THE WITCH OF BLACK ISLE
THE SCOURGE OF BLACK ISLE
THE GHOSTS OF BLACK ISLE
THE GIFT OF BLACK ISLE

THE CLAN GRANT SERIES
#1- RESCUED BY A HIGHLANDER-
Alex and Maddie
#2- HEALING A HIGHLANDER'S HEART-
Brenna and Quade
#3- LOVE LETTERS FROM LARGS-
Brodie and Celestina
#4-JOURNEY TO THE HIGHLANDS-
Robbie and Caralyn
#5-HIGHLAND SPARKS-
Logan and Gwyneth

HIGHLAND SWORDS
THE SCOT'S BETRAYAL
THE SCOT'S SPY
THE SCOT'S PURSUIT
THE SCOT'S QUEST
THE SCOT'S DECEPTION
THE SCOT'S ANGEL

THE SOULMATE CHRONICLES TRILOGY
#1 TRUSTING A HIGHLANDER
#2 TRUSTING A SCOT
#3 TRUSTING A CHIEFTAIN

STAND-ALONE BOOKS
ESCAPE TO THE HIGHLANDS
THE BANISHED HIGHLANDER
REFORMING THE DUKE-REGENCY
WOLF AND THE WILD SCOTS
FALLING FOR THE CHIEFTAIN-3RD in a collaborative trilogy
HIGHLAND SECRETS -3rd in a collaborative trilogy

THE SUMMERHILL SERIES-CONTEMPORARY ROMANCE
#1-ONE SUMMERHILL DAY
#2-A FRESH START FOR TWO
#3-THREE REASONS TO LOVE

ABOUT THE AUTHOR

Keira Montclair is the pen name of an author who lives in South Carolina with her husband. She loves to write fast-paced, emotional romance, especially with children as secondary characters.

When she's not writing, she loves to spend time with her grandchildren. She's worked as a high school math teacher, a registered nurse, and an office manager. She loves ballet, mathematics, puzzles, learning anything new, and creating new characters for her readers to fall in love with.

She writes historical romantic suspense. Her best-selling series is a family saga that follows two medieval Scottish clans through four generations and now numbers over forty books.

Contact her through her website: *keiramontclair.com*.